Her friends would understand. They'd vowed on graduation day to have it all—love, marriage and children.

And Tori, well, she had Jeff. He didn't love her. She was going to have his baby and he didn't know. The situation was all messed up.

"You'll be late," she told him, impatient to get him out of the office. "And I have phone calls to make."

"Oh. Okay." He moved toward the door, as if reluctant to believe that she would really send him away. After all, how many times had she caved over the years?

"Call me if you change your mind about us." And with that he was gone, the door clicking shut behind him.

Tori put her head in her hands. She'd made it.

She'd seen him…and survived.

Dear Reader,

Two of my best friends are single mothers. One was in her twenties, engaged at the time she got the news. My other friend was in her early thirties, and she found out she was expecting after she'd already broken off the relationship. Both knew the road ahead would be difficult, and they have done a phenomenal job raising their respective boys.

You may remember Tori, Jeff's girlfriend from *Unwrapping Mr. Wright.* Tori's just received nine months' notice that her life is about to change in a major way. Not only is she starting a new career in a new city, but she's also going to be a single mother. She's ready to do this alone, but Jeff has other, better ideas. Long ago Tori vowed to have it all upon graduation (career, husband and family), and Jeff's determined to make her dreams come true, even if not quite in the order she'd planned.

I hope you enjoy *Nine Months' Notice*, the final book in my AMERICAN BEAUTIES miniseries. I had a great time writing Tori's story. (Lisa's was *The Marriage Campaign;* Cecile's *The Wedding Secret.*) This book marks my fourteenth for Harlequin Books and I can't state enough times how grateful I am that you, the reader, have been with me all the way.

As always, enjoy the romance and feel free to drop me an e-mail at michele@micheledunaway.com.

Happy reading,

Michele Dunaway

Nine Months' Notice
MICHELE DUNAWAY

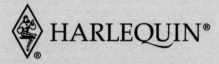

HARLEQUIN®

TORONTO • NEW YORK • LONDON
AMSTERDAM • PARIS • SYDNEY • HAMBURG
STOCKHOLM • ATHENS • TOKYO • MILAN • MADRID
PRAGUE • WARSAW • BUDAPEST • AUCKLAND

ISBN-13: 978-0-373-75162-4
ISBN-10:   0-373-75162-1

NINE MONTHS' NOTICE

www.eHarlequin.com

Printed in U.S.A.

ABOUT THE AUTHOR

In first grade Michele Dunaway wanted to be a teacher when she grew up, and by second grade she wanted to be an author. By third grade she was determined to be both, and before her high school class reunion, she'd succeeded. In addition to writing romance, Michele is a nationally recognized high school English and journalism educator. Born and raised in a west county suburb of St. Louis, Michele has traveled extensively, with the cities and places she's visited often becoming settings for her stories. Described as a woman who does too much but doesn't know how to stop, Michele gardens five acres in her spare time and shares her life with two young daughters, six lazy house cats, one dwarf rabbit and two tankfuls of fish.

Michele loves to hear from readers. You can reach her via her Web site, www.micheledunaway.com.

Books by Michele Dunaway

HARLEQUIN AMERICAN ROMANCE
988—THE PLAYBOY'S PROTÉGÉE
1008—ABOUT LAST NIGHT...
1044—UNWRAPPING MR. WRIGHT
1056—EMERGENCY ENGAGEMENT
1100—LEGALLY TENDER
1127—THE MARRIAGE CAMPAIGN*
1144—THE WEDDING SECRET*

*American Beauties

Don't miss any of our special offers. Write to us at the following address for information on our newest releases.

Harlequin Reader Service
U.S.: 3010 Walden Ave., P.O. Box 1325, Buffalo, NY 14269
Canadian: P.O. Box 609, Fort Erie, Ont. L2A 5X3

For Lisa & Jenni.
You go, girls.

Prologue

Tori Adams was nobody's fool, except maybe when it came to Jeff Wright. She might have an excuse once a year for letting her boss be her pied piper, but that didn't excuse the other 364 days. Eight years ago, when she'd started her new job at Wright Solutions, you could rationalize her infatuation by calling her young. Just out of college. Naive.

They'd worked together for six years before she'd given in to her desires and mixed business with pleasure. The relationship had a rocky start, but, like baked Alaska after the fast flare, everything had calmed down.

They'd settled into a monotonous, dead-end rut.

Not that each time they were together wasn't delicious. Take last night. All he'd had to do was touch her, something as simple as running a fingertip along the top of her arm, and she was molten and ready. Bottle his magnetism and she could make a fortune and retire twenty-two years early.

Of course, love was like that. Unfortunately, their love was strictly one-sided. Hers. Jeff had made it perfectly clear time and time again that this was as far as the relationship was going to go.

But that didn't alleviate the fact that she'd fallen hard and held every man she'd met since against the impossible Jeff-standard. Even if George Clooney and Matthew McConaughey showed up on her doorstep, they, too, would fall woefully short.

As for Jeff, he was a man content with the status quo, oblivious to her growing frustration. He was satisfied with their current situation, which was to get together every Saturday night, so long as neither was traveling. They were monogamous. Committed.

In a very twisted sense, Tori thought wryly, for unlike those hot and spicy romance novels that ended with the hero and heroine finding happily-ever-after, Tori knew that, in her case, the reality was that her relationship wasn't going anywhere. Ever.

She loved him, which is why she saw him at every opportunity, no matter how much her heart shredded slightly each time she did. He did care for her—she had no doubt of that—but his feelings would never reach that death-do-us-part, you're-my-forever level that she craved. Their love was physical. Surface. And after two years, Tori wasn't even sure Jeff had deep emotions beyond the ones everyone has for his immediate family. The man simply didn't get angry. He played life loose and took things as they came. He shed stress the way a roof sheds water—easily.

She'd learned the hard way that you should never go into a relationship expecting to change a man. You were only going to leave disappointed.

She'd settled for less than body and soul, something she swore long ago she'd never do. Why had she given up hope of finding something or someone better? When had the tiny part of her that believed she could have it all died? She loved Jeff, but not everything you loved was good for you. Just look at cheesecake. She'd eat that daily if it wouldn't pack pounds on her hips. She'd never been afraid of the unknown, but something about Jeff had paralyzed her into complacency and made her lose sight of her dreams.

She'd lost her backbone. She'd even agreed to spend the weekend with him when she knew she should have stayed home and concentrated on getting well. She'd been on antibiotics the past seven days for a spring sinus infection. She had three more days of medication remaining, and still went from being totally stuffed up one moment to nonstop sneezing the next.

But she hadn't seen him in a week and she missed him and… She glanced at the clock before she slid out of bed. Eight-fifteen. Her nose twitched as she stilled a sneeze, and she took a moment to stare at the rumpled bed where Jeff lay sleeping on his stomach, the sheet slipped to his waist. He was a gorgeous man—even more handsome than his twin, Justin. Jeff had light-green eyes, unlike his brother, whose were more emerald. Jeff's chin rounded more than Justin's squared one, and Jeff's Roman nose had been broken during a long-ago hockey game, giving a roguish quality to his face. His hair was the perfect shade—not too red or too orangey-blond. Not one freckle from childhood marred his skin.

Even asleep he tempted her. Maybe she should just climb back into bed and…

She shook her head, snapped herself out of it, and gathered up her stuff. She headed into the en suite bathroom of Jeff's condo. She'd leave in a few minutes while he was still sleeping, as she did most of the time. Sundays were Jeff's sleep-in days and Tori, who was always up by eight no matter what the day, actually preferred to have the afternoon to herself so she could get ready for the week ahead.

She freshened up and crammed the last of her personal items into the small white bag she carried between his place and hers. As she did, her fingers settled on the little plastic case that contained her birth control. Frowning, she popped it open. She hadn't taken last night's dose. Twelve hours shouldn't make a difference; she'd forgotten before.

She pushed a pill out and popped it into her mouth, swallowed and sneezed. High time to go. Within minutes, Tori was inside her car where the letdown came immediately. She couldn't keep doing this indefinitely. She wanted more. She'd made a vow with her friends at graduation to have it all and if she stayed in St. Louis in this situation with Jeff, her life would be over before it started. In the harsh late-April sunlight, Tori finally admitted that she'd reached her limit. Something had to change.

Chapter One

There were two pink lines on the plastic stick. Tori stared at the pregnancy test she was holding in her right hand as if willing it to change. Even though she had a master's degree in computer science, she held the test up to the back of the box to make sure she'd read the results correctly.

Two lines. Pregnant.

The box gleefully proclaimed that it was 99.9 percent accurate, but Tori read the wording again. The odds she was pregnant were pretty good; this was the second test she'd taken—the first one she'd wrapped in layers of toilet paper and stuffed back inside the box about five minutes ago.

That test had also been positive, which meant she wasn't just missing her period because of stress as she had done a few times before in her life. As she'd thought had happened at the end of May. No, two months of missed cycles and two positive tests meant one thing.

She was having Jeff Wright's baby.

Tori wrapped the second stick in toilet paper and shoved it into the box before placing the whole package back into the plain brown bag the drugstore had thoughtfully provided. She tossed the sack in the trash can, making sure to hide it at the bottom.

She hadn't planned on taking the test, especially not at work. She'd run by the drugstore at lunch to get some headache medicine and, worried about having missed her period twice in a row, had picked up the test after she'd passed it in the aisle. Then the box had sat in her purse like a homing beacon. Finally, at about four o'clock, she hadn't been able to take the suspense any more. She had to know the results.

And now she did.

She straightened and took a long, hard look at herself in the mirror. She was about to be a mother. While a woman had reproductive choices today, Tori had known the moment she'd bought the test what her decision would be if the results were positive.

She gazed into her own brown eyes. While this wasn't quite how she'd planned it, she knew she would be a wonderful single mom. She was turning thirty December first; she had a good job with excellent benefits; and, as a fantastic "aunt" to her friend Joann's kids, Tori knew she could handle diapers and feedings. Besides, her whole family lived near Kansas City, where she had recently moved, giving her a great support system to draw on. And she knew that her best friends from college, the Roses, would agree with her and support her decision.

Still, the irony mocked. While she'd been trying to change her life by moving to Kansas City and breaking up with Jeff at the end of May, she certainly hadn't intended this.

Tori blinked and shook her head. She'd recently shed her long, dark hair, chopping off six inches so that the locks now bobbed just below her chin. She wasn't quite used to not having the weight and the strands tickled her chin.

She sighed. Taking the test was probably going to be the easiest part. Despite all her book smarts, she had little idea how to proceed. Did one just call up and announce, Guess what? I'm pregnant? Was there a chain-of-command of people you were supposed to tell first, such as your own parents or the father? Did it even matter?

Even the decision to accept the promotion and transfer to Kansas City had been easier to make than facing the situation now looming on the horizon.

She thought about her new job a moment. Her career had always been a top priority in her life, and relocating had let her leave Jeff behind. She hadn't seen him since leaving St. Louis, and time had been a healing balm, giving her much-needed space and perspective. Oh, she still loved him—part of her always would—but she wasn't moping anymore. She'd put the past behind her and was ready to start a new life. She'd joined some of the women in the office in their Internet dating adventures. While she hadn't found anyone, at least she was back on the market.

Although not for long. She was going to have a baby.

How would Jeff take the news? Would he be excited? Or would he feel inconvenienced, trapped? She'd been on the Pill and they'd never discussed the possibility of kids.

Tori swallowed the hurt that often rose when she thought of both Jeff and her past failure in not accepting the hopelessness of her situation earlier. Deep down she knew that his first love was his job; he focused on work and the endless travel that came with it. He and his brothers, Jared and Justin, had founded Wright Solutions, a technology company that did everything from designing and installing high-end networks to selling software to hardware recycling and disposal. Jeff and his brothers had made Wright Solutions a one-stop shop for business computing needs.

Of the three brothers, Jeff was the problem solver, which was the trait that had first attracted Tori. He stopped hackers, recovered data, and strengthened firewalls. He was focused—like her.

When she'd first been hired, she'd worked in his division. Their paths had diverged when she'd been promoted, and now everything Wright Solutions touched west of Kansas City was handled through her office. The management position was a crowning achievement. Her salary and stock options let her live comfortably.

When she'd broken things off, she'd been determined not to let her personal life interfere with her career. She had no intention of changing companies and jeopardizing her future advancement. She and Jeff had been friends first; surely they could be friends post-breakup.

Now a wrench had been tossed into the machinery. She put her hand on her still-flat stomach. He'd make beautiful babies. He had the right to know. She winced. She had no desire to tell him. She would, of course, but only after she saw the doctor and made sure the tests were correct.

Tori backed away from the sink. Oftentimes, she'd wondered if she'd made life too easy for Jeff—maybe that's why things had never progressed. Unlike most couples, they talked only in person, keeping in touch via short e-mails, Jeff's preferred means of communication. He wasn't a phone conversationalist and all their calls lasted less than five minutes, unless they were fighting.

Not that they fought often since, really, there wasn't much to argue about. From the beginning, Jeff had been clear on how their relationship was going to be— monogamous, hot, passionate, no strings, easily ended whenever the other felt like it.

Never once had they discussed children, much less marriage. She'd told Jeff how she felt about him once, but he hadn't replied in kind. He'd told her he liked things how they were. Instead of walking away as she should have done—and isn't hindsight twenty-twenty?—Tori hadn't pressed, accepting that something was better than nothing. She should have left him long before she had.

Now the writing was on the wall or, more aptly, the lines were on the stick. Tori Adams, who had graduated summa cum laude and who could solve complicated math problems in her head, had blown it. Just as she had been poised to start over, to find someone to spend her life with, the traditional life she wanted—find the guy, get married, have children—she was about to get exactly the opposite. She'd always be tied irrevocably to Jeff. They'd always share a child.

A knock sounded on her outside office door and Tori opened her bathroom door and called out, "Hold on."

She made sure the remnants of her tests weren't lying around, washed her hands and closed the door behind her. She gave her office one last glance to make sure nothing was amiss, then double-checked her Friday casual outfit for lint before she greeted her visitor.

Jeff Wright stood in front of her, a wide grin on his face. "Surprise."

"JEFF," TORI SAID, her equilibrium rattled. She suddenly felt like the neurotic, guilty man in Edgar Allan Poe's "The Tell-Tale Heart." She took a deep breath to calm her nerves; there was no way Jeff could know her secret and she refused to blurt out her news here. "Jeff, what are you doing here? Did we have an appointment?"

Jeff frowned, the grin slipping from his face. "No, we didn't have an appointment. I didn't know I needed one. In fact, I'm not really visiting, I just have a fast layover before flying back to St. Louis."

He closed her office door behind him, the click audible. "I figured I'd pop by, check out the KC office. See how you were doing. We haven't talked in a while."

Tori stared at him. "Well, I haven't seen you since I transferred and I report to Justin now," Tori said, trying to get a sense of why he was here unexpectedly. This was out of character for him.

Jeff shifted his weight from one foot to the other as if the situation wasn't going quite the way he'd envisioned. "Everything okay with the job? Still like it?"

Tori nodded, her hair dancing around her chin. "It's been great. We've landed five new accounts and exceeded all of last quarter's income projections."

Jeff stuffed his hands into his pockets for a moment. Tori had never really liked wearing heels, and in her flats he was seven inches taller than she was. "I guess I should have asked if everything is okay with *you?*" he clarified.

"Why wouldn't it be?" Tori asked, forcing herself to relax. She'd tell him about the baby after visiting the doctor, when she would know things such as her due date. Now was not the time.

"No reason." Jeff raked a hand through his strawberry-colored hair, a habit whenever he was nervous. "I guess I just miss talking to you. Maybe things aren't okay with me."

He missed her. She could see it reflected in his eyes. Maybe they had a chance. Maybe…

"I've really missed you," he repeated. "I want you back in my life. It's been weeks."

While her body hummed with the longing it always felt around Jeff Wright, his subsequent statement had made her want to fall through the floor with disappointment. He didn't love her. He was just sexually frustrated. They'd never had problems in that department.

She was determined that this time she wouldn't succumb to his charms or his "needs." She was going to be a mother. Time to grow up and stop living in fantasyland. He wasn't going to change.

"I can't see you anymore," Tori managed, proud of herself for keeping her chin up and somehow looking him in the eye. They'd fit each other once, but no longer. He was a man married to his computer and his cat. She wanted more than an addiction she slaked every week. She wanted it all, like the love her mother had found with her second husband, Tori's stepfather. "I'm sorry, but no. It's high time for both of us to move on. Although I would like for us to be friends."

Jeff stood there, his pale-green broadcloth shirt making him look sexier than any model. The imaginary devil on her shoulder screamed in her ear that she was being an idiot. But deep down she knew this was the right thing to do. She wasn't aware she was holding her breath until she exhaled at the exact moment he slowly said, "I see."

An awkward silence descended. Tori's body still hummed; the man was as irresistible as chocolate cake—but she was winning the battle against indulging. "I know this sounds harsh, but we always said we'd let each other know when we were ready to move on. I'm happy here. New town, new life."

"New man," Jeff said, his tone edgy.

"Eventually," Tori confirmed, knowing that finding a man was now the lowest item on her priority list. Her baby came first. "We're at opposite ends of the state. We've always been friends—we can put things back the way they once were. That would be best."

"Yeah, I guess we can be friends," he said, his watch beeping as the alarm went off. He silenced it.

"Work?" Tori said.

"Always. I need to get back to the airport," Jeff said. "I'm flying to St. Louis and then tomorrow I'm headed to Buffalo for a week-long project. After that I'm home for a little while before I'm back out in L.A."

"You do travel a lot," Tori observed. She knew that he'd racked up over half a million frequent-flier miles the year before.

Jeff grinned, but this time his smile didn't quite reach his eyes. "Yeah, well, you know how I like to be constantly on the go. I like the adventure. No grass grows under my feet."

She did, which was why she held her tongue and simply gave him the patient smile of one ready to get back to work. He recognized the message and stepped toward the door. "I guess I'd better get going. Airport security's tight right now and I don't want to miss my flight."

"Probably a good idea," Tori said, doing her best to hold herself together for a few more minutes. She could let him go, let him walk out without breaking down. Seeing him was hard, but she had to remember that he hadn't changed. This visit confirmed the futility of her current situation. She was having his baby, and part of her would always love him, but he'd never love her. And to top it off, he was always working and jetting off somewhere. The job would always be number one, not her or the baby.

Jeff paused. "Should I tell Lauren you said hi?"

Tori nodded. "Please."

Lauren was Justin's wife and she was currently on maternity leave. Over three years ago, she and Tori had been on the company Christmas-party committee together and they had been friends since. That night had been a catalyst for both women's relationships with the Wright twins.

Tori suddenly realized she'd have to take a six-week maternity leave at the very least. She made a mental note to check her company benefits brochure. A bit overwhelmed by all the changes she was facing, Tori moved to sink into the sofa located in her office.

"You appear a little pale," Jeff said. "Can I get you something to drink before I go?"

"I'm fine," Tori said, waving him off. "Go catch your flight. I'll get something later."

He didn't seem to believe her. "You're sure?"

"Yes." What she needed was for him to leave.

"Let me get you some water anyway," Jeff said. He strode to the small bar fridge in the corner. "Have you been eating?"

"Yes. Plenty," Tori said, watching him. He'd always

been kind to her, remembering things such as her favorite foods. She focused. That didn't mean he loved her.

"So, do you still talk to your friends in St. Louis?" Jeff asked as he gave Tori a bottle of water.

"Yes. Lisa's getting married. She called to tell me last week. I'm still in shock."

"Lisa's one of your sorority sisters," Jeff said. He dallied for a moment.

"Right. Rho Sigma Gamma."

As she spoke the words, Tori felt a slight twang of depression. She, Lisa Meyer, Joann Smith and Cecile Deletsky had pledged together and become fast friends. Joann was a stay-at-home mom of three. Lisa was a po-litical fund-raiser working on getting her candidate into the Missouri governor's mansion. Cecile had relocated to Chicago and was a producer for a popular talk show. They'd been extremely supportive of Tori's decision to leave Jeff. She wondered what they'd think when she told them her news.

At least that would be easier than telling her own mother. Her mother was going to be, in a word, *disappointed.*

Her friends would understand. They'd all vowed on graduation day to have it all—love, marriage and children. So what if Tori wasn't doing things in order? Of course, while Joann had been pregnant when she got married, she'd at least had a man who loved her.

Tori, well, she had Jeff. He was now standing beside her, a reminder that for her, dreams didn't come true. He didn't love her. He wanted her for sex. She was going to have his baby. The situation was all messed up.

"You'll be late," she told him, impatient to get him out of the office. "And I have phone calls to make."

"Oh. Okay." He again moved toward the door as if finally believing she meant to send him away. Or maybe it was because he had a plane to catch. How many times had she caved over the years? He popped a piece of gum into his mouth. "I can't miss my flight. I'll see you later. Call me if you change your mind about us."

And with that he was gone, the door clicking shut behind him. Tori trembled and placed her head in her hands. She'd made it. She'd seen him and survived.

Chapter Two

"What are you still doing here? Don't you have a date?"

Jeff glanced up from where he'd been staring at the flat-screen computer monitor, a confused expression on his face as he looked at his twin brother. "Date?" he echoed. He hadn't had a date since Tori dumped him. Not that he couldn't have had someone else in a snap, he consoled himself. There was that girl on the flight to St. Louis. But he'd walked off the plane without her phone number. Work was a priority and, frankly, Tori's defection and her subsequent rejection had rattled Jeff a little more than he realized. Even now it bothered him.

As for dates, his calendar was clear until tomorrow when he had to fly across the state to St. Joseph for a business meeting. He didn't have anything on the agenda except to go home and play the latest video game of which he had an advance copy.

Justin rolled his eyes and exhaled a sharp breath. "You are useless, you know that? You have a date with Hailey. Remember your niece?"

"Oh—" Jeff bit off the expletive and jumped to his feet. He pressed a button, closing all programs and sending the computer to sleep. "Sorry. I got so busy fine-tuning tomorrow's presentation that I forgot all about babysitting."

"Yes, my wife kind of figured that, so here I am."

Justin crossed his arms and Jeff cringed at his oversight. "Time just slipped away from me."

Justin nodded. "It always does, which is why Lauren was wise enough to call and ask if you were buried up to your eyeballs in work. She also said if you get over there pronto maybe she'll forgive you."

Jeff grinned. Lauren knew him far too well. They'd been next-door neighbors in the same condominium complex until she'd married Justin. Now, Jeff was an uncle and he relished the role. But as always, he'd got caught up in a project and had forgotten the real world. While his dedication was fantastic for the company, it played hell on earth with his personal life. He was always late—or at least 96.5 percent of the time. Drove most people nuts. Tori had been the exception.

Jeff sobered at that thought. He really needed to stop thinking about her. They'd promised each other that neither would dwell on the past. If she was moving on then he had to respect that. Even if she was one of the few people on the planet who truly understood him.

Jeff was a numbers person—a math savant if you wanted to go that far. He'd taken calculus in the eighth grade, college courses during high school. He loved to search for numerical patterns. Computers fascinated him. Give him a technological task and he was like a dog with a bone. The rest of the world seemed to disappear.

But he always eventually returned to reality. Like now. He stood and headed toward the door. Playing uncle, even with dirty diaper changes, was quite a good time, much more interesting than a lot of visits with other relatives he endured once a year. He'd discovered that Hailey already had him wrapped around her little finger. Ten months old. Who knew a woman's power started so early?

"Call Lauren and tell her I'm on my way," Jeff told Justin. He grabbed his briefcase. "You guys don't live far, so she'll still have plenty of time to run her errands."

"Thanks," Justin said. "Lauren really wants to get out of the house. She's got some things to do and Mom can't babysit today. Lauren doesn't want to take Hailey out in this heat."

Jeff nodded, understanding. Even though summer had barely started, St. Louis was already suffering a miserable streak of 100-degree days with little chance of rain. Even the grass had turned brown and everyone's air conditioners were fighting to keep up. Without a good rain, the rest of the summer was going to be lousy.

Jeff arrived at his sister-in-law's about ten minutes later. "Hey, Lauren. Sorry I'm late." He gave her a quick kiss on the cheek as he stepped into the foyer of the one-story house. Jeff immediately reached for his niece. "How's my little boo?"

Lauren rolled her eyes at Jeff's pet name, but Hailey didn't seem to mind. From the security of her mother's arms she lunged forward and reached both hands out for her uncle. Jeff caught her. As soon as he had Hailey securely, Lauren stepped back and let go.

Jeff walked into the living room carrying Hailey. His niece smelled of baby powder and that fresh, sweet scent synonymous with little girls. Lauren had probably given her a bath.

Jeff glanced at Lauren. Her blond hair was pulled up in a ponytail and woven through the back of her white St. Louis Cardinals baseball cap. In shorts and a T-shirt, she looked every bit the suburban mom.

"So get shopping," he told her. "I've got this down. Is the formula still in the same place?"

Jeff bounced Hailey slightly and his niece laughed. The television was on in the corner of the room, tuned to a children's show on PBS. Jeff put his hand under Hailey's back and said "Airplane!" Then he swooped her slightly, as if using her body to draw the bottom of a bowl. Hailey shrieked, and Jeff grinned as Lauren tried not to wince. "Giving Mom a heart attack, aren't we?" Jeff teased. "Paying her back for probably doing it to her parents."

"Yeah, well," Lauren said. She watched for a moment before giving a resigned shake of her head. "The formula's in the cabinet and I just washed the bottles. Call me if you have any problems."

Lauren reached for her purse and Jeff followed her into the kitchen. Because she'd walk through the utility room into the garage, he'd parked on the street so she'd be able to back out easier.

"Go. I'm fine here," Jeff commanded.

Lauren was always hesitant about leaving Hailey, especially now that her daughter had just started walking. Hailey was one of those babies doing everything early, just as her daddy and her uncle had.

"You know I've got her," Jeff insisted.

"I know you do," Lauren said. She looped her purse strap over her arm. Content with Jeff, Hailey didn't cry even as her mom headed out the door. Lauren paused a moment. "You know, you'd make a good dad. You should think about having one of your own. Give Hailey here a cousin or two to play with as she gets older."

Jeff's cheeks heated and he knew his face probably matched his hair. "Well, I… Jared's taken care of that," he said. His older brother did have two children already.

"Good save," Lauren said. "By the way, what's going on with you and Tori? You dated her longer than anyone else."

"Yeah, well, things change," Jeff said. "This here is the only girl who has my attention right now. I guess Kansas City is too far away to make anything work." Hailey laughed as Jeff gave her a raspberry on her belly.

Lauren frowned, the small crease between her brows indicating she wasn't done with the topic. "So what if she's in KC? Last I checked that wasn't very far away, a four-hour drive tops in that speedy new Corvette you just bought. And I know you have plenty of frequent-flier miles you could use. I mean, if you want something to work, distance shouldn't be a factor. Perhaps you should go after her. Women like that. Justin chased me and see how happy we are?"

"Don't you have somewhere to be?" Jeff prodded, not really wanting to discuss Tori. He wrinkled his nose and his expression soured. "You know, Lauren, you're welcome to stay and linger if you'd like to change your lovely daughter before you leave."

Lauren shook her head and laughed. "No, no, I'm going. That diaper can be your penance for being late." She opened the door to the garage. "Remember, call me on my cell if there's a problem."

"Will do," Jeff promised. He held Hailey easily as he took her back to her bedroom and placed her on the changing table. She gazed up at him, her green eyes

wide. While she'd inherited her dad's eyes, the pale
downy hair coming in was definitely from her mother.

"You are a pretty thing," Jeff told her. "You'd have
to be for me to change you. I'm pretty discriminate
about whose diapers I take off. You know, I never
changed any of your cousins. Don't tell them, okay?
They might get jealous."

Hailey simply blinked at him. She was still a little
too young to say actual words—those would come in
another month or two, followed by incessant conversation at eighteen months.

Jeff folded up the diaper and tossed it into the trash.
"I won't bore you with the statistics on how that diaper
will take more than five-hundred years to degrade," he
said. Hailey continued to wait as Jeff wiped her bottom,
added some baby powder, then securely fastened her
new diaper. Within seconds, she was back in his arms,
her cute pink dress draped over his arm.

"So what do you think? Did I do an okay change?"
As he walked back into the living room, Jeff thought
about what Lauren had said. He liked the idea that he'd
make a good father. He loved Hailey and even though
Jeff and Justin were twins, Hailey could tell them apart.
Stand Jeff and Justin next to each other and she wanted
her dad every time.

Perhaps babies simply made you feel paternal. For
a minute Jeff reflected on the fission of happiness that
had shot through his system when Hailey had reached
for him. Was the moment exponentially better and more
powerful when it was your own child? Jeff had no idea,
but holding Hailey felt right. Maybe he was getting to
the place in his life where he was ready to settle down.

"Who knew guys had biological clocks?" Jeff mused

aloud as he placed Hailey in her exerciser. While he might have doubted it a few years ago, he knew now that he wanted to be a father. Of course it took two people for that. Had he committed a cardinal sin somewhere along the line with Tori? They'd been so comfortable together and then all of a sudden, boom, she'd moved to Kansas City and broken up with him. He sighed. On the TV screen a blue puppet was singing about the letter *H*.

Hailey was happily playing and safe, so Jeff mulled over the conundrum. He'd known Tori for what amounted to forever. She'd outlasted any other woman in his life aside from his mother. He and Tori had been friends for years before they'd first gotten together after the company Christmas party. Their passion had been hot and fast, but the next day she'd told him it had been a mistake and had gone back to her ex-boyfriend for a few weeks. He'd chased her then, won her and then they'd developed a routine. He cared about her more than anyone else.

But was she the one? Jeff sat there a moment, distracting himself by watching Hailey spin around in her exerciser. How did somebody know he'd found his soul mate? Justin had screwed things up terribly with Lauren and almost lost her. Jared hadn't had things easy, either. Sure his brothers were happy now, but neither had had a lightbulb "aha" moment at the start of their relationships. And love wasn't like installing a software program. There were no signs that you were one-hundred percent complete.

As for compatibility, he and Tori thought the same. They were both math people who had taken extra math classes in school just for fun and to boost their GPAs. They were long beyond such trivialities as wooing and making an impression. She knew how much he cared about her and he the same. Actions spoke louder than words, which could often be meaningless, any day. Tori's last boyfriend had told her he loved her and then cheated on her right and left. Jeff hadn't wanted to make that same mistake, so he'd erred on the side of caution.

In his job, he was the one who traced problems back to their source. He found solutions, made sure the situation never crept up again and, if it did try to rear its ugly head, he made certain that it could be quickly eradicated. So had he missed something? Had he been too conservative? Had he taken Tori for granted? A squeal interrupted his reverie. Hailey had stopped spinning and was looking at him with a dazed but satisfied expression. She held out her arms.

Jeff rose and went to get her. "Up you go." She snuggled next to him, ready for a bottle and a nap. He ran a hand over her downy hair, marveling at its blond softness as he carried her into the kitchen. He knew Tori well enough to know that she was through with him. Jeff had blown it with Tori big time. But his brothers had each found their perfect mates. Proof was right in his arms—a life created out of love. Maybe, if he was lucky, there was still hope for him.

Chapter Three

The day before her first doctor's appointment, Tori was unable to shake the mixture of melancholy and excitement she was experiencing. On one hand, she was thrilled to be becoming a mom. On the other, she already felt overwhelmed—think of all the preparations she had to make. The phone rang and Tori picked up on the second ring.

"Hey, stranger," Tori said, having recognized Cecile's phone number on the caller ID display.

"Hey, yourself," Cecile said. "I haven't talked to you in ages. What's up?"

"Everything," Tori admitted. "I—"

"Ah, Jeff," Cecile interrupted. "What's going on with him? You haven't gone back to him, have you?"

"No," Tori said. She chewed on her bottom lip. "He did stop by the office once."

"And?" Cecile prodded. A few seconds of silence later Cecile said, "Oh."

"No, not that," Tori replied. "I held my ground. I told him it was over."

"That's good," Cecile said.

"Maybe," Tori agreed after a moment. She opened

her mouth to tell Cecile about her doctor's appointment when Cecile said, "I met someone at my sister's wedding reception."

"Really?"

"Yeah," Cecile said. "Hotter than the summer day. Blond. Tall. Body to die for and more magnetism than the north pole."

"And what's wrong with that?" Tori asked.

"I imbibed," Cecile admitted. "I said I wasn't going to and I did anyway. So much for turning over a new leaf."

Tori winced. "Will you see him again?"

Cecile sighed. "I don't know. He's my brother-in-law's best friend. I'm sure our paths will cross. I didn't leave a number and I'm still debating if that was the right thing to do."

"You got me," Tori said. "That's sort of what happened with me and Jeff. We got together one night and I regretted it afterward. Maybe I should have trusted my judgment."

"Debatable," Cecile said. "You cared for him. It was an easy mistake—you shouldn't beat yourself up over it."

"I guess. Things are a little weird right now, especially since I still work for him. This job's so good, though, I wasn't going to give it up for something less."

"And you shouldn't have to," Cecile said. "Wright Solutions is a great company to work for."

"Exactly. Still, it's hard. I keep believing that if I don't think about him it'll get better. I mean, I'm not afraid of being alone."

She wasn't because she had plenty of friends and work to keep her busy. But moving on was still difficult, she was letting a part of her life go. Jeff had been her present and—she'd hoped—her future, and now he was her past. Sort of.

She'd always have a little piece of him now that she was having his baby. She wasn't sure if that was good or bad, but it didn't matter. It simply was.

"Cecile, what would you do if you found out your one-night stand left you with a baby? Would you tell him?" Tori asked, moving into her kitchen and grabbing a plastic cup.

"Why are you asking me this? Did you have a one-night stand you didn't tell me about?"

"No," Tori said, holding the cup under the ice dispenser. She wanted Cecile's honest answer before she told her about the baby. "Hypothetical. I just wondered if you'd tell him."

"In my opinion, children should grow up having two parents if that's possible," Cecile said. "But I guess it's hard to say when it's not happening to you."

"I suppose there's no easy choice," Tori said, sipping her water. For some reason she felt slightly dehydrated.

"Why all this interest in this topic? You're not pregnant, are you?"

Yes.

Tori opened her mouth to say the word but at that moment Cecile's phone beeped, indicating she had another call. "Hey, that's my mom. She and Dad are letting me take one of their old armchairs for my apartment. Do you mind if I answer them and get back to you later?"

"No, that's fine. We'll talk soon. Call me anytime." Tori hung up and glanced around her apartment. She'd splurged, getting a one-bedroom loft unit with upgraded appliances. On the first floor she had a living room with a fireplace, a kitchen, a washer/dryer and a half bath.

Upstairs she had a full bathroom and a bedroom that overlooked the living room. Her apartment, which had seemed so spacious when she'd first moved in, wasn't going to be adequate once she had the baby.

She walked over to the refrigerator and pulled off the magnetic to-do notepad she'd hung there. She grabbed a stray pen she found on the breakfast bar and, standing, she wrote at the top: Go to doctor's appointment. Underneath she wrote: Decide what to do about Jeff.

Disgruntled, she sighed, set the paper down and finished drinking her water. She debated about what Cecile had said. What type of a father would Jeff be? He was never in town. He hired a pet sitter to care for his cat. How could he be a dad if he was always traveling? The man had no focus unless it was technology related. Babies were about as basic as things came. They couldn't talk, walk, feed themselves or communicate. They needed nonstop care. She worried that Jeff wouldn't be able to handle the work involved, even if he did babysit Hailey now and then.

Long ago, when she'd first gotten into the relationship, she'd dreamed of what it might be like to be married to Jeff Wright. She'd quickly realized that it wouldn't be the stuff of romance novels. While they were compatible in tons of ways, in reality she and Jeff had stayed together because they didn't worry about things such as who was doing laundry, who was paying for what and who was doing his or her fair share. They'd neutralized the issues married couples dealt with. She'd wasted two years trying to make something work; she and Jeff didn't have staying power—that deep commitment and determination to get through things beyond just pleasure and convenience.

Tori put her glass in the dishwasher. When she'd been eleven her parents had divorced. Her dad had moved to California. She'd seen him only on rare occasions and heard from him when he'd remembered her on major holidays. She wouldn't allow her child to have that type of life.

People might argue that a child deserved two parents, but Tori thought a child deserved two parents who made the child a top priority. If that weren't possible, then no parent was better than one who constantly made you wonder whether you were worth it or whether you were valued at all.

If Tori wondered about her place in Jeff's life, what would her baby think growing up, asking where Daddy was and why Daddy "forgot"?

Tori tapped her fingers on the countertop, the background noise a comforting staccato. Her own mother hadn't gotten remarried right away, waiting instead until the perfect man had come along when Tori was a sophomore in high school. Richard Kennedy was the perfect stepfather. Tori's mother had never been happier. And Richard had always made Tori feel valued and welcome, even when she'd become a big sister. Although Tori was almost sixteen years older than her younger brother, Kenny, the two were close. The whole family was close. That was all to Richard's credit.

Tori reached for her phone and pressed a speed-dial button. Within seconds, her mother picked up. "Hey Mom," Tori said. "When's the next family dinner?"

"You trolling for a free meal?" her mother, Kathleen, teased. "Tomorrow's Friday and Kenny's got a baseball tournament this weekend so we'll be over in Raytown.

Of course you're welcome to join us if you're not heading to St. Louis."

"I might be," Tori lied.

Her mom was used to Tori's travels. "How about Monday, then? After work? Say six o'clock? We're all off for Independence Day, so we can relax."

Tori wrote the information on the sheet of paper she'd been using. "I'll see you then. Love you."

"Me, too. If you change your mind, call me. I know Kenny would love to see his big sister at some of his games."

"I'll see what I can do. Maybe next weekend. E-mail me the schedule and I'll work something out."

"I'll do that. Talk to you soon. Love ya."

"Me, too." Tori ended the call and strolled into the living room. Her apartment backed up on to woods, and her living room windows overlooked nothing but old oak trees. When out on her balcony, she could pretend she lived in a tree house. She'd signed a year's lease, but would have to find somewhere else to live when it expired. Something one-story with few steps that would need to be gated off. Maybe she'd buy a condo.

Why had she told her mother she was heading to St. Louis for the weekend? Tori had never considered herself a chicken, but, once she'd called her mom, she hadn't found the nerve to tell her about the baby. At least the story gave her a bit more time to figure out how to tell them.

So maybe she was a bit of a chicken. She'd never been afraid of anything before, accepting any challenge put before her. In college a boyfriend had dared her to go bungee jumping, knowing Tori had a fear of heights.

Refusing to back out, she did it and never showed how scared she really had been. Tori wasn't afraid to get down and dirty when necessary.

At least, she used to be fearless. Her life was changing so fast that suddenly she felt timid. Unsettled. Not quite herself. She wasn't invincible any longer. She couldn't just jump in feet first and worry about the consequences later. Tori placed her hand on her stomach, something she'd been doing constantly, as if touching herself somehow made the fact she was going to be a mother real. She knew she couldn't hide from what was happening. She'd see the doctor, make sure everything was okay and there were no complications and then tell Jeff. That would be the best, most prudent course of action. She'd then tell her family and friends. After all, there was still a point-one chance the test could be wrong.

"YOU'RE DEFINITELY PREGNANT," Dr. Sarah Hillyer said as she moved the ultrasound wand over Tori's stomach, pressing slightly. "If you look right there on the monitor, that's your baby. While it's not much yet, this is the outline of the head and this is the body."

Tori's breath caught in her throat. The black-and-white image wasn't the sharpest, but she could make out what the doctor was showing her. *There was life growing inside her.*

"We'll schedule you for another ultrasound before you leave today," the doctor continued. "You'll see a whole lot more then as it will be a more in-depth examination. This one just tells us that you aren't going to be having multiples. You said the father was an identical twin and twins do run in families. From what I can tell, you're just having one."

"Wow," Tori said simply, taking a final peek at the screen before the doctor removed the wand from her stomach.

"Quite incredible, isn't it?" Dr. Hillyer said. "I see so many of these and I'm moved every time. Go ahead and get dressed, then meet me in my office."

With that, she left the room and gave Tori her privacy.

Tori sat up and used the paper towels provided to wipe the gel off her stomach. Despite the positive pregnancy tests, Tori had still wondered if they hadn't been wrong. The ultrasound, though, sealed it for her. She was going to be a mother. Although the image hadn't looked like much, she was having a baby and it was depending on her for nourishment. She'd never been so happy or so humbled.

She dressed and went to the doctor's personal office. Dr. Hillyer was already seated behind her huge mahogany desk. "Based on when you were taking the antibiotics for you infection and on the results of the ultrasound, I'm estimating your due date to be December 30. You just might have a New Year's or a Christmas baby. All the doctors in our practice deliver their own babies, and I will be in town that week." She grinned. "Try not to have it on a holiday, though, okay?"

"I'll try," Tori said, sensing the doctor was joking. Babies showed up when they chose and Tori had every intention of delivering naturally.

"Good. Here's a prescription for prenatal vitamins. This next sheet I'm giving you is a list of the hospitals I deliver at. Most of them schedule tours of their maternity wards, so you'll want to go visit them and decide which one you like best. Then let me know and we'll get you pre-registered. That's done about two months in advance."

Dr. Hillyer handed over another sheet. "This one is a timetable of your office visits. I'll see you once a month, then, as the date gets closer, we'll schedule the appointments every two weeks, then weekly until the little one arrives. This last sheet is simply a list of symptoms to watch for. If you experience any of these, call my office immediately. Got that?"

"Got it," Tori said. The doctor handed her a folder to put everything in.

Dr. Hillyer smiled. "Then, unless you have any other questions, you're free to go. My nurse is Eileen Swikle. Ask for her whenever you call, and she'll answer any questions you might have over the next six months. She'll become your best friend through all this."

"Thanks," Tori said. She stood. "For now I'm good. Slightly overwhelmed, but good."

"Understandable," the doctor said with a nod. "First pregnancies are a learning experience. After that, the next one is a piece of cake. And you should know that you have no restrictions—sex, travel, working out. You're free to indulge. Just remember no alcohol or smoking."

"I don't smoke and gave up drinking," Tori said.

"Good girl," Dr. Hillyer said, and with that, Tori was on her way to the scheduling desk, where she made her appointments through October. There was a moment when she turned a little queasy; the receptionist had a sliced turkey sandwich on her desk and for some reason the smell set Tori off. The woman quickly put it aside when she saw Tori go a little green.

Armed with her vitamin prescription and her folder, Tori left the office. As she stepped out into the afternoon sunshine, she sighed as the enormity of her pregnancy hit her. She'd seen her baby. This was actually happening.

Even though there had been definite lines on the pregnancy test, maybe the logical part of her hadn't quite believed the results. The heat enveloped Tori as she hit the remote and unlocked her two-seater sports car. She loved the little convertible but she was going to have to trade it in for something more practical.

She slid onto the warm leather and ran her fingers across the steering wheel. She'd have to buy something with a back seat. She cringed as a minivan drove by the parking lot. No. She just couldn't drive a minivan. Not yet. Surely there had to be something less "suburban mom." She made a mental note to start researching what was out there.

Although it was hot enough to want to turn on the air conditioner and hide from the sun, Tori lowered the convertible top. She figured she might as well enjoy her toy a little longer. Her cell phone rang, and despite Jeff's statistical lecture on why not to use it while driving, she popped in the earpiece and hit the connect button.

"Hey, I finished all my shopping, so I'm running early—I'm already here. Are you on your way?" Lauren asked.

"I just finished my last appointment, so I can head in that direction now," Tori told her. Lauren had called last night and announced she was coming into town a day early for her aunt's sixtieth birthday party. "Did you find a gift?"

"I did," Lauren said. "It took me about five stores, but I finally found the right thing. This is the first real shopping I've done since having Hailey. A trip to the supermarket just doesn't count."

"I'm getting on the highway now. I'll be there in

thirty minutes, tops." Tori accelerated, letting her hair blow as she made her way toward Country Club Plaza, Kansas City's premier shopping area. Lauren was staying with her aunt, who lived nearby. Tori navigated the route easily and soon sat across from Lauren in one of the Plaza's restaurants. The two ordered and were soon munching on appetizers as they discussed how Hailey was doing.

"Jeff says hi," Lauren suddenly said, sliding in her words at a break in the conversation.

"Tell him I say hi, too," Tori said, working to make her voice casual. She wasn't sure how much Lauren knew. "Except for work, I haven't seen him in a while."

"He said you two were just friends now," Lauren admitted. She watched Tori's face carefully, looking for revealing expressions, but Tori remained matter-of-fact. "I wanted you to know that I hope you and I can always remain friends."

"Of course we can," Tori insisted. She took another bite of her salad and waved her fork in the air. "It's better this way. Relationships just don't work out when you're in two different cities. Besides, it was probably time for both of us to move on."

"It's good you two can be friends," Lauren noted.

"We were always friends first," Tori said. At least that much was true. She took a drink of her water. Lauren was having a glass of wine and she took a sip, rolling the merlot she'd ordered over her tongue.

"Enjoying that?" Tori said, realizing that it would be at least another nine months before anything alcoholic touched her lips.

"Oh yes, I am," Lauren said as she took another sip. "I never drink anything but water when I'm out with Hailey, so being out with another adult female means I can indulge a little." She stabbed a piece of the thinly cut beef that topped her blue-cheese-and-steak salad. "This is good," she said. "And the company is great, too."

"Thanks," Tori said. "You gave me an excuse to get away from the office." With Lauren's visit and the doctor's appointment, Tori had taken the afternoon off.

"So how's work?" Lauren asked.

"We won a major contract to redo Fredrikberg Finance's network. They're a loan brokerage with ten offices all over the city. We haven't had a glitch during the procedure, but their president calls me every day anyway for reassurance."

"Well, you look healthy," Lauren said. "You've got a glow about you I haven't seen before, so Kansas City must be agreeing with you."

"It is," Tori said. At least her job was.

After having dinner last night, Tori had decided to bite the bullet and tell her mother and stepfather about the baby.

Surprisingly the conversation had gone quite well. They'd quickly hidden any disappointment that there wasn't a husband to go along with the baby and offered whatever help she required. When she thought about it, Tori realized her parents were quite excited they were going to have a grandchild.

So far she'd told no one else, although she now decided to call her friends. She still hadn't decided what to say to Jeff. Tori took another bite of her salad. She'd given up all fattening foods the day of the pregnancy test, opting for only the healthiest things available. When she felt hungry, she munched on saltines or rice cakes. She missed chocolate-chip cookies terribly, but she was determined not to swell up to the size of a hot-air balloon.

"Earth to Tori," Lauren said.

"Sorry," Tori said. "My mind has been processing so much lately that sometimes it just shuts down."

"I was like that when I was pregnant," Lauren said. "It was as if, in utero, Hailey was absorbing all my brain cells. Justin called me a flake."

"He didn't," Tori said, laughing.

"He did," Lauren admitted with an expression of mock horror. "I only let him get away with it because he indulged all my strange cravings. I would want fried pickles, for instance, and he'd drive to O'Leary's and get them. He'd even get me Ted Drewes or Fritz's con-cretes at all odd hours. I also craved mashed potatoes and fajitas. The poor guy didn't have a home-cooked meal for months."

"I don't cook very much, and I can't stand sliced turkey anymore," Tori said. "I just look at it now and want to puke." Although the ice cream treats Lauren had just mentioned sounded heavenly.

Lauren's expression turned quizzical. "I was that way with scrambled eggs. I couldn't even be in the same room and smell them."

"I'm fine with eggs," Tori said, before she caught herself. What was she doing discussing cravings with Lauren, who didn't even know she was pregnant? Now she had to use the ladies' room. While she'd heard trips to the bathroom became more frequent as the baby grew, maybe it was also psychological. Or perhaps it was due to the eight glasses of water she consumed every day. "Excuse me a second," she said, rising and heading to the restroom.

When she returned, Lauren was staring at her strangely. "So why haven't you told Jeff you're expecting?" she asked.

"What?" Tori slid into the seat and paused. "I'm not pregnant."

"Then what would you call it?" Lauren asked. She pushed her blond hair behind her ears. "You forget that both my aunt and my mother work for obstetricians. I can spot a pregnant woman a mile away."

Tori winced. She should have kept her mouth shut about her cravings.

"So, which doctor are you seeing?" Lauren asked.

"Dr. Hillyer," Tori admitted, willing herself to keep her eyes open. At this moment she wanted nothing more than to close them and hide from the impending cloud of doom. Dropping through the floor was another option, if the tiles would be gracious enough to open up.

"When are you due?" Lauren asked.

"December thirtieth."

"And Jeff's the father and he's in the dark," Lauren continued.

"I just had my first visit with the doctor today," Tori said. She fiddled with the cloth napkin. "I wanted to be sure I was pregnant before causing any undue excitement. You know how many things can go wrong in the first trimester."

"You have to tell him," Lauren said. She twirled her wineglass between her fingers, the red liquid swirling. She frowned before adding, "He has a right to know."

"Yes, I know he does. And I will tell him," Tori said. "Just not yet. I want to get a few other things sorted out on my end. But I promise that I'll speak to him. Sometime. It's better this way."

"For who? You?" Lauren shook her head. "The longer you wait the worse it's going to be. At some point he's going to find out. He's not stupid. He's quite able to put two and two together. And can you imagine how he's going to feel? He'll want to be involved from the very beginning. You'd be keeping his child away from him."

"It's my child, too," Tori said. "I want things sorted on my end first."

"Yes, but you should allow him to be involved. He's like his brother that way. Justin went to my checkups. He visited the hospitals with me. He went to my sonogram appointments and held my hand when I gave blood. He did the grocery shopping when I was too tired. He even organized and helped fix up the nursery."

"I can do that on my own," Tori said stubbornly. "I've been taking care of myself for years and I'm sure I'll be fine doing it pregnant. You and I both know that Jeff is much too busy. He's out of town as we speak. He's a nomad. I don't want that life. I'm not settling for a man who's never around. He and I talked long ago about our relationship—he wants sex, I want marriage. He's admitted he's not ready to settle down and pretty much indicated that if he were, it wouldn't be with me. He doesn't see me that way. I'm keeping my baby, but I'm not having it to trap him. The last thing I want is to win Jeff Wright because of his misguided sense of guilt."

A silence fell for a few moments. "I'm sorry if that sounded harsh," Tori said. "I have a lot on my plate. I agree he should be involved, but we're over. I need to be the one to set the parameters of how involved he's going to be. I'm not going back to the way it was."

"And I can respect that," Lauren said. "I believe a child should know both parents even if living together isn't in the best interests of the parents."

"In this case, it wouldn't be good for either of us," Tori said. "I was moving on with my life when this happened. I'm simply praying that Jeff will understand that we shouldn't be together."

"You don't think he'll make a good father, do you?" Lauren asked, as if she'd gained sudden insight into the workings of Tori's mind.

"No, I have to admit I don't," Tori acknowledged. "I want what my mother has. I want what you and Justin have. Jeff, well, he's got two priorities—work and his computer. You thought you were in love with Jeff once. You know exactly how single-minded he can be. It's like he has tunnel vision."

"I do know, and what I felt for him was a misguided crush," Lauren said, clarifying the situation. "Justin quickly straightened me out. Okay, not so quickly. But Jeff and I aren't compatible. You and he are. All of us can see that. You're perfect for him."

"Only because I put up with his nonsense longer than anyone else," Tori said.

"Perhaps," Lauren agreed. "But he talks about you all the time. I know he cares about you, and cares deeply."

"He does care," Tori said. "That's never been an issue. But he cares for me the way he used to care for you—in that just-friends sense, only with me sex was added. While we may be great in bed, that's not enough to make a marriage."

"But what if he loved you?"

"He doesn't. And I want the kind of love and affection that you and Justin share. The kind everyone can see. That's not us. We didn't do anything but sit around and watch movies. We were a couple, sort of. I'm tired of sort of. That's why I called off the relationship and accepted this promotion. I want a husband who adores me and I can't have that with Jeff. I need to take off the blinders so I can search for the right someone— someone who will be there forever. I'm not settling or marrying anyone until I've found that."

"If you could see Jeff with Hailey, you wouldn't even recognize him. He's so good with her. She practically jumps out of my arms when she sees him," Lauren defended.

"She probably thinks he's Justin," Tori said skeptically. She bit her lip. "Sorry. That was mean."

Lauren shook her head. "It was, but I'll forgive you because it's a valid point and I worried about that myself. They are uncannily alike, but Hailey knows the difference. When they're in the same room she goes to Justin and says Dada. She knows who Jeff is and who he's not. You can tell that she loves her uncle very much, but she adores her father."

Tori settled back against the chair. While deep down she wanted nothing more than the unconditional belief that Jeff would make an excellent father, he was terrible at expressing his feelings. "Yes, but Jeff's great one-on-one like that. He keeps everyone in a certain compartment. He's not with a child constantly. It's like when he's with me. We're great in short bursts, but long-term, all day, every day? We'd be hating each other by the end of two weeks and that's if we were lucky."

"I think you'd be surprised. I thought life would be that way with Justin, but it wasn't," Lauren said. The two women had finished eating and Tori waved away the waiter's offer of dessert.

"I'd like to be surprised, but I don't believe I will be," Tori said. "There's too much history between us. The last thing I want is for us to marry and end up hating each other. Good things come to those who wait. I'm not afraid of being alone until the right man comes along."

"You won't be alone. You'll be a mother," Lauren pointed out.

"True," Tori said. And her family had promised to help and support her. Even though she wouldn't be in a relationship, everything was going to be fine. "I will tell him soon," Tori promised. "Just say you won't speak to him before I do."

"Fine," Lauren said. "I won't. But if you don't tell him in a few weeks, expect a phone call from me. This is not a secret I like keeping, but because we're friends and have been since long before I married Justin, I'll give you some time to sort things out. I can understand you wanting to make sure you've got your own thoughts straightened out, but don't wait too long. You need to let him know before he finds out from someone else. You'll be showing soon. Office workers talk. Don't make him find out through the grapevine."

"I won't," Tori assured her. "Just a few more weeks and I'll figure out a way to tell him."

"I'm going to hold you to that," Lauren said. The matter settled, Tori and Lauren talked about other things until the check arrived, hugged each other goodbye and promised to keep in touch.

It wasn't until Tori was in her car that she realized

the full extent of her mistake. She'd been so intent on making sure Lauren didn't tell Jeff, Tori had forgotten all about his twin. Lauren hadn't promised not to tell Justin. Tori had to hope and trust that Lauren's promise extended to her husband as well.

HER PHONE RANG as she merged into traffic on the way home. "Hi, Lisa."

"Hey!" Lisa said. "I'm not catching you at a bad time, am I? I wanted you to know that Mark and I set a date. What are you doing the second weekend of August?"

"Coming to St. Louis?" Tori guessed. "Walking down the aisle?"

Lisa laughed. "Yes on both counts. I need you for the first two weekends in August, if you can get away from the office. There's a shower for me the weekend before the wedding and we're getting married the next. The reception is at Mark's parents' house. You don't have a Neiman-Marcus department store in Kansas City, do you?"

"I'll check the Web site, but right now I'd say no."

"Rats. You'll love the dresses and don't worry, they're really reasonable. Anyway, Cecile's getting measured at the store on Michigan Avenue, so why don't you come here? How's this weekend?"

"I'm actually going to be in St. Louis next Monday for a meeting with Jared. How about we meet after that?" Tori suggested. "I'm coming in on Sunday anyway."

"Only if you come in earlier so we can do dinner, too," Lisa said. "Joann's going to be in town this weekend, as well, so we can all get together like old times."

"Twist my arm." Tori laughed. "You know how much

I like to eat. So put this Sunday on your calendar and send me an e-mail confirmation. I should remember, but I'm driving and don't have a hand free to pencil it in."

"That's why you sound like you're in a tunnel," Lisa said with a chuckle. "I'll do it right now. So will you be bringing anyone new to the wedding?"

"No," Tori said. "Haven't met anyone."

"Well, Mark has some single friends who are flying in. One of them can serve as your date. Just as friends. No matchmaking."

"Only if you promise."

"Still doing the Internet dating thing?" Lisa asked.

Tori put her blinker on and switched lanes. "About to give it up. I never found anyone interesting. E-mail me all the information about the dress and the wedding events and I'll put it on my calendar. I'll see you this weekend."

"I'll do that today," Lisa promised.

"You're happy, aren't you?" Tori asked.

"Very," Lisa said, not missing a beat. Tori could hear the contentment in her friend's voice.

"Good," Tori said, satisfied that Lisa had made the right choice. She wanted nothing more than for Lisa to be happy for the rest of her life.

Tori disconnected and hit the on-ramp for the highway. This weekend she'd tell both Joann and Lisa about the baby. She hadn't wanted to tell Lisa over the phone. She knew her friends well enough to know that face-to-face chats were always best for news such as this.

Chapter Four

"You're kidding me. I did hear you right, didn't I? You're pregnant."

Tori averted her gaze and toyed with her iced tea, using the long spoon to create a tiny whirlpool in the tall glass. She was sitting in the Meyers' four-season room, surrounded only by Joann and Lisa. Instead of dining out, Joann's husband, Kyle, and brother, Mark, who was also Lisa's fiancé, had barbecued. The men had since gone inside to watch the Cardinals baseball game, leaving the women to socialize.

Joann gazed at Tori. "You cannot go silent now. My ears are not shot from having kids. I believe you said you're pregnant."

"I did," Tori said slowly. "You heard me correctly. Nothing's wrong with your ears."

"No, but something is wrong with your mouth. You didn't say anything to us until today," Lisa jumped in. "How long have you known? You should have called when you first suspected."

"How far along are you?" Joann asked. She'd lifted her water goblet to her lips.

"My due date's December thirtieth," Tori said.

"Oh my God," Lisa said, her jaw dropping as she worked the math. She frowned. "That means you got pregnant—"

"Back in April sometime," Joann finished. She tapped her glass with a manicured nail. "That's an awful long time ago. I'm sure you had quite a few opportunities to spill the beans and share what was going on."

"I know," Tori said. She crossed and uncrossed her legs. She wore shorts and a casual sweater.

"So, spill," Lisa commanded. "We're a little disappointed that we're finding out weeks later so you better tell us why and how—all the details. We're your best friends. We could have been there for you."

"Right," Joann said. She brushed some lint off her camp shirt. "That's the real reason we're all so frustrated. We haven't been able to be a part of this with you. We've already drifted so much, and it's news like this that keeps us together."

"I didn't even know until I was about eight weeks along," Tori said, which was the truth. Her friends nodded, encouraging her to continue. "I had some spotting after the first four weeks and then no period after the next month. That's when I finally went and bought a test. Stress has thrown off my cycles before and I had just moved to Kansas City and, well, after the test I wanted to wait until I saw the doctor before I announced anything. I didn't want to be like Alicia." Tori mentioned one of their sorority sisters.

"I remember that. She thought she was pregnant, went out and told everyone and then the doctor said she wasn't," Lisa said. "She cried for days."

"She did get pregnant the next month, though," Joann

noted. "She and her husband had been trying for a while for a child."

"Well, I didn't want that to happen to me. I knew for sure the day you called me to tell me the wedding date," she said, nodding at Lisa. "But I decided to tell you in person instead."

"Okay, we understand. We're still going to dish out maybe a smidgen more guilt for you having kept us in the dark, but you know we're only doing that because we love you."

"Yeah," Tori said, her insides warming. Her friends were always there for her.

"Besides, this gives us something to do after the wedding. We'll have to do baby showers and shopping and such," Lisa added.

"I haven't even thought that far ahead," Tori said. "I'm still crying from having to give up my cute convertible at some point in the near future. I asked fate for change, but this isn't what I was expecting when I broke up with Jeff and moved to Kansas City. Nothing has gone the way I planned."

"Trust me, I can empathize," Joann said. "Finding out I was pregnant was very intimidating. I mean, here I was about to move away and take a job as a news broadcaster. I was on the verge of starting my career. Worse, I was leaving Kyle behind. Oh, sure, we'd planned to do the long-distance thing—"

"That doesn't work out," Tori said.

"—exactly." Joann nodded. "Deep down I believed it was the beginning of the end for us and I was only fooling myself thinking otherwise. Then I found out I was pregnant, which I knew wasn't going to sit well with my new employers. So what did I do? I loved

Kyle, but I wasn't sure giving up my career was what I wanted. And was Kyle ready to be a dad? We were about to be parents, and we were just out of college. The last thing I wanted was for him to think I was trapping him. Worse, if I became a stay-at-home mom, was I disappointing my parents who had such high hopes for me and had paid for my degree? There were no easy answers. I felt like I'd made such a mess of things."

"I know what you mean," Tori said. "Call it the ostrich syndrome—I want to stick my head in the sand long enough for all of this to go away. I know it won't, but I still want to pretend that I'll wake up and everything will somehow be okay. Really, I need to give myself a good, swift kick in the pants."

Joann took a sip of water. "Tori, that feeling's normal. But the first step is to stop beating yourself up. Trust me when I say that it will all work out. In my case, my life changed for the better. I love being a stay-at-home mom. I have a few projects in the works that I can do from home. Sure, there are times I envy you girls and your exciting careers, but I wouldn't throw away what I have for anything."

"Of course not," Lisa said, reaching over to pat Joann's hand. "Honestly, all of us have envied you, too. Our careers don't keep us warm at night. Marriage and children do. Who wouldn't want that?"

"Me?" Tori said, her hand shooting up. "This was unplanned. Jeff doesn't love me and I won't be marrying him because of some misguided moral code. There are no legitimacy issues these days."

"So you're planning on being a single mom?" Lisa asked.

"I am," Tori said. "I'm keeping my baby. I'll love this

child. I love him or her already—though I'm not too thrilled about the morning sickness."

"It should go away eventually," Joann said.

"And we're behind you one-hundred percent," Lisa said. "Cecile will be, too. So does Jeff agree with your decision?"

Tori twisted the linen napkin she had her lap and prepared to reveal her last secret. "I haven't told him about the baby yet," she admitted.

"Haven't told him," both her friends echoed.

"No, I haven't. He doesn't know." She straightened. "I'm afraid Jeff will immediately think he has to be chivalrous. That's the last thing I want. When I get married, I want it to be with a man who loves me. When the time's right, I'll let him know. I mean, I'm not going to be able to hide the pregnancy. We work together—sort of. And as much as I would love to keep my figure, I doubt I'm going to be one of those women who doesn't look pregnant. If genetics are any indication, I'll be just as big as my mom was during both of her pregnancies. She supersized with Kenny. I doubt I'll be able to convince everyone I've suddenly got fat."

"Now I understand why you asked Cecile those questions a while ago," Lisa said. "She told me about it." Lisa filled Joann in on the phone conversation Tori and Cecile had had. "Tori, what are you going to do? Are you planning on telling Jeff?"

"Eventually," Tori said stubbornly. "While I believe Jeff has a right to know, I don't want him sweeping in here and demanding to marry me because of some misdirected principles. He doesn't love me. He's said he doesn't want more. If I tell him, I could make things worse."

"Or better," Joann said hopefully. "I believe a dad has a right to know, but then I'm biased because of Kyle."

"Your situation was different. Kyle loved you."

"True," Joann said. "Even though I don't necessarily understand your choice, you know I'll stand behind you and your decisions. We'll keep your secret for as long as you want. You can trust us. I'm sure Cecile would say the same thing."

"I know I can trust all of you," Tori said. Her friends' words were their bond. It was unbreakable. Tori felt tears in her eyes.

"Here come the hormones," Joann said sympathetically. "I cried over everything. Still do. Especially those Hallmark commercials."

"I should have told you about the baby earlier," Tori said. "It's been hard dealing with this, even before I took the test. I've felt like an automaton, like I've been in a permanent state of shock. All of a sudden I'm scared. I don't know what to do or how to proceed. My life isn't my own. I have so many decisions to make and there are no simple answers. I want to put some things in place before I call him and break the news."

"Is there a possibility he might find out some other way?" Lisa asked.

"Lauren knows, but she told me she wouldn't say anything to Jeff if I told him within a few weeks," Tori said.

"That's good," Lisa said.

Tori sat there a moment. "Before I forget to say this, I'm so glad I have all of you to help me through this. I'm not sure what I'd do without you guys."

"Of course you have us," Lisa said, before she got up and came around to stand behind Tori. She put her hand on Tori's shoulder. Joann reached over and grabbed one of Tori's hands.

"We'll always be here," Joann said. "You know that. No matter what."

"I'm going to get as big as a house. I'll probably be fat for your wedding." Tori sniffled.

"No, you won't," Lisa said. "You aren't going to gain that much by mid-August."

"I hope not," Tori said, reveling in the strength emanating from her friends. "I'm lucky to have you."

"We know," Lisa said. "Now tell us what you need us to do."

SHE WAS LUCKY she had such great friends, Tori thought as she opened the door to her apartment. Funny how fate brought you the people you most needed in your life. She was truly blessed. She'd barely put her purse on the counter when her cell rang. She recognized the number.

"Hey, Lauren. What's up?"

"I—I'm so sorry, but Justin knows. I didn't mean to tell him but it just came out. I wasn't planning to tell him. I swear."

Tori closed her eyes, praying that Justin now wouldn't announce the news to Jeff.

"I know. Just slow down," Tori said. While dread was consuming her, she had to be rational about this.

"Justin has a sixth sense when something's bothering me. I didn't mean to say anything, but he sort of guessed. I've asked him not to tell Jeff, but I don't know if he'll keep this to himself. He wasn't happy that you were being quiet, but was also pretty annoyed with Jeff. He called his brother a few choice names, the nicest of which was moron."

"Ouch," Tori said. She could almost envision Justin's reaction. She sighed. "Lauren, don't worry. I understand—you're married, and husbands and wives shouldn't have secrets. I shouldn't have put you in that position. I wanted to get some details ironed out before I told Jeff—you know he's going to expect us to get married."

"He was raised to do what he thinks is right," Lauren said.

"I know," Tori said. "But in this case, that's not it. Not when he doesn't love me."

"Which makes him an idiot," Lauren said. "On that I agree with Justin." In the background Tori heard a small cry. "That's Hailey. I've got to run. I'm sorry. If I can help to soften the situation, don't hesitate to call."

"I won't," Tori said, hanging up. She glanced at the calendar hanging on her kitchen wall. She was suddenly out of time.

"JEFF WRIGHT is here to see you," Tori's receptionist informed her through the phone's intercom. It was Wednesday afternoon, only days since Tori's luncheon with her friends and Lauren's call. He hadn't waited long.

"Hi, Tori," Jeff said as he walked into the room and locked the door behind him. "Surprised to see me?"

"Not really," Tori replied, trying to sound nonchalant even as her dread grew.

"Didn't think so," Jeff said. His cheek twitched, indicating his anger. Tori winced.

Once Lauren had called, part of Tori had been relieved that the decision of how to tell Jeff had been taken from her. While she'd planned on calling him at the end of the week, deep down she knew she should have done it sooner. She'd made matters worse by keeping things from him.

"I just have one question," Jeff said bluntly. "Why didn't you tell me you were pregnant? Should I not have been the first to know? Why did I have to hear about it from my brother, who found out from his wife?"

"I intended to tell you. I was going to call you and ask you to meet with me at the end of this week," Tori said, the words sounding lame and unsympathetic in her ears. Her reasons for waiting until she was prepared had seemed right, but now with Jeff glaring at her, she found herself mired in self-doubt.

"Hadn't gotten around to it?" Jeff appeared ready to explode. He calmed himself. "Tori, you're carrying my child. Let me tell you what I think we should do. Let's get married."

He paused and when she didn't answer, added, "Don't be stubborn, Tori. It's the right thing to do."

She bristled. Jeff was acting true to form, and Tori readied her rebuttal. "No, it's not. We don't live in the dark ages. Stop acting like a caveman."

Tori pressed her back firmly up against her leather office chair, her posture rigid. She had to admit she found his anger oddly exciting—she'd never got under his skin like this before. She forced herself not to blink as she stared into his green eyes.

"Tori, a child needs two parents. The best thing is for us to get married."

"Our child *will* have two parents. You and me," she said. "But we aren't getting married. And don't even think that if you keep badgering me I'll change my mind. You know me better than that."

For one brief moment, Jeff looked shocked. But he quickly regained control over his emotions and squashed them like a bug. Tori knew he was assessing the situation, the same way he did when he played chess or attacked a computer problem—taking his time. She bit the inside of her lip.

The silence lengthened and while Tori sat there she found herself mentally tracing her fingertips over his eyebrows, recalling their smooth texture. Her imaginary roving fingers forged a path over each silky wisp, down his jagged nose and lingered at his lips.

She shivered; the desire she always had for Jeff made her legs clench as her body betrayed her. Pregnancy certainly hadn't changed her hormones. The absence of his touch had made her feel like a starving man who saw food that he couldn't have. Thinking about touching those brows and kissing those lips was a fantasy she shouldn't be having. Her back aching, Tori shifted, trying to find comfort in the chair.

Jeff exhaled his frustration. He ran a finger beneath the collar of his short-sleeve polo shirt. "How long have you known? Did you know before you took this job that you were pregnant?" he asked.

She shook her head. She owed him this much. "No, I didn't. I've missed cycles before and I thought it was nothing important. I saw the doctor last week, right before I met Lauren. That's when I knew for sure. I'd planned on calling you this week."

Jeff began to pace the length of Tori's office before he made a grand, sweeping gesture with his right arm, the arm he'd often curled around her as they'd slept. "I don't understand how this happened," Jeff said, his expression stricken. "I mean, I understand *how* it happened, but you were on the Pill. We've never had any problems before."

She and Dr. Hillyer had talked about this. "Yes, I was on the Pill, but I had been sick and stressed out with a sinus infection so I was taking antibiotics, not realizing there was a slim chance they could decrease the effectiveness of the birth control."

"Yeah, it did," he said. He cringed at the harshness of his statement. "That came out wrong. Sorry. I'm just still so shocked by this, although that's no excuse. So where do we go from here?"

"Nowhere," Tori said. "My salary is more than enough for me to support our child and my benefits will cover everything. I'm fine. We'll work out something."

Jeff stopped pacing abruptly and took several steps toward her desk. "Do you really think so poorly of me that you would assume I don't want to be involved in this?"

His hypnotic stare held hers, and his deep voice rumbled as he continued in that low and husky tone that always made her flush, always made her immediately ready no matter what they were discussing. "We had something good together. I care about you. Would marrying me be that bad?"

Despite her staunch stand, excitement began to bubble through Tori. If nothing else, her body had missed lying next to his. Their lovemaking had been nothing less than phenomenal, and various parts of her ached for the man whom she'd stopped seeing yet still hadn't been able to put out of her mind, especially after discovering she was pregnant.

Could she ever escape Jeff Wright? She'd been trying and had thought she was on the right track, but a baby meant she'd be tied to him for eternity.

Picking up a pencil gave her a way to break out from under his spell, the yellow wood a solid reassurance beneath her trembling fingers.

"Jeff, what we had wasn't a forever kind of relationship."

He leaned forward and placed his hands on her desk, bringing himself within kissing range. Tori's heart raced as heat rushed through her, the adrenaline pulsing to her now curled toes. For some reason a line from *Star Trek* came into her head— "Resistance is futile."

But she would resist. Despite her physical reaction to him, Tori refused to back away.

"I want to be a part of our baby's life, Tori."

"And you will be," she said, noticing his breath smelled of spearmint.

"No, not like this. My son or daughter is not going to have to ride in a car to come see me once every two weeks or something. I want to be there all the time."

She opened her mouth to speak, but, seeing his expression, closed it again. Jeff inhaled sharply before continuing.

"I know this isn't the undying-love type of marriage proposal you wanted, and—" he shook his head "—of course I know I'm no longer the man you want, but we have a child to consider."

He straightened and paced for a moment, as if gathering his thoughts. "I only want to do what's best."

He returned to stand before her desk. Needing space, Tori scooted her chair backward. His intense gaze had affected her. Her fingers tightened their tenacious grip on the pencil.

Of course Jeff wanted to do what was best—he was an honorable man. But she wanted it all; that meant holding out no matter what. "I won't marry you," she managed.

"Why not?" he shot back.

"You don't love me and I won't marry without love."

There. The words were out. His eyes widened and she could read the truth there. Her heart broke.

A strange tiredness ringed Jeff's eyes. Finally he spoke. "We're good together. We can be friends like we were. I'll make sure of it."

Tori rested her hands on her stomach, the pencil still in her tight grasp. "Jeff, you can't promise that. Emotionally, we're miles apart in what we want from this relationship."

His calm facade fell. He slowly stretched his fingers one by one. She realized the unflappable Jeff Wright had snapped like a taut string. He was fighting for her. Unfortunately, his actions came way too late.

The irony almost made her cry, but a quick, painful chomp on the inside of her cheek made the tears stop. She reminded herself that Jeff was like a drug—even now she wanted to have it—but loving him wasn't good for her. If she succumbed, she'd eventually be left alone with a man whose priority would always be work. They'd play house but never share the deep emotional connection other married couples had. And while there would always be that part of her that dreamed of being his wife, she wouldn't marry him for convenience and she wouldn't settle. She glanced up at him and saw the proud, determined man she had once loved with reckless abandon—so much so that she'd denied being true to herself.

Relying on every ounce of strength she had, she said what she needed to, even though it pained her to do so. "Jeff, you're wasting your time and I know how much you hate that."

"You are never a waste of my time. Never." His lips drew into a tight line. She itched to soothe him, touch his face, kiss his lips as she'd once done long ago....

The pencil in her fingers snapped in two as he strode to the door and said, "I have a business engagement, so I need to leave. But this isn't over."

As soon as Jeff left, Tori exhaled. It felt as if she'd been holding her breath since his unannounced arrival at her office. She tossed the pencil fragments into the trash can and wiped the graphite residue off her fingers.

She rubbed her temples to calm her nerves. Once again his work had interfered, proving to her he wasn't ready to be a father. For once, she was grateful that his job had called him away, but she knew he'd return. He'd proposed. He'd marry her—even if he didn't love her.

Pushing her emotions aside, Tori pondered Jeff's appearance. He'd changed. While he still looked fantastic, he had seemed haggard today, as if the endless treadmill of work was finally beginning to beat him.

Then again, just because she worked at the same company didn't mean she saw him enough to know if her assessment was right. This was only his second visit since the breakup. Maybe the shadows under his eyes had been a trick of the light. His lips, though, had been the same. Full, perfect and eminently kissable. She'd wanted to kiss him. As she contemplated that, she let her shoulders slump forward.

"Hey, Tori, are you all right?" Darci Evans asked.

Concern etched her receptionist's face and Tori worked to give her a reassuring smile. "Don't worry, I'm fine."

Darci's gaze was skeptical. "Everyone in the office

is worried about you, Tori. You know you're more than our boss—we're family here and you've been really pale lately. All of us agree that you're working way too hard. Wright Solutions isn't worth your sanity."

Tori sighed. It was a close office, with everyone being more of a team than a hierarchy. "That's not it. You might as well know, since I'm sure the secret's going to get around very soon. I'm pregnant."

"You're what?" Darci stood there, flabbergasted.

"You heard me correctly and, no, I don't want to talk about it today. Just keep this to yourself for now, okay? I'm not done sorting it out but I'll make an official announcement soon. Please. I'm trusting you with this."

"Okay," Darci said. "I won't say anything. You know me well enough to know that I won't."

"I do," Tori said.

"So can I assume the baby is Jeff's by the way he stormed out of here?" Darci asked.

Tori nodded.

"Whatever you do, don't let him upset you. You have a baby to take care of."

"Believe me, I'm not," Tori said. "But enough about this. Did the fax I need come in?"

"It did." Darci handed it over and they talked for a few more minutes before Darci left. Tori leaned back in her chair and she momentarily closed her eyes, enjoying the quiet. It wouldn't be long before Jeff made good on his word and returned. He wasn't going to back down. Well, neither was she.

Chapter Five

"You look like you've been sucker punched."

"It's hot outside." Jeff walked into the two-bedroom hotel suite, sidestepping his best friend, Clint, and reaching for the bottle of beer that Clint was handing him. "Thanks. It's been a difficult day."

"Tell me about it," Clint said. He had been Wright Solutions' vice president of public relations, Lauren's boss. When Lauren had had Hailey, Justin hadn't wanted to hire anyone to replace her. About the same time, Clint had left the company to form his own PR firm. The situation worked out for everyone as Wright Solutions immediately began outsourcing their PR to Clint.

Clint was in Kansas City to do a trade show for one of his other clients, and Jeff was grateful that fate had given him a friendly face to see and a place to crash during this trip. The two had been friends since high school and they often played Friday-night poker together. Needing someone to confide in, Jeff had told Clint about Tori's pregnancy within hours of his arrival in KC. "So the show was good?" Jeff asked, avoiding the subject of his meeting with Tori for a moment.

"It was a full house, and our booth really stood out. We had nonstop traffic and generated tons of interest. I guess my hard day was the good kind, though. I'm assuming this afternoon didn't go well?"

Jeff strode to the window, leaving Clint's question unanswered. The hotel offered a spectacular view of Kansas City's Union Station, and the horizon to the west. Jeff finally turned around to face Clint, glad he had someone to share this with. "No, she's not being very cooperative," he said. "She said no to marrying me."

Clint winced. "Sorry."

"No, I'm the one who's sorry," Jeff replied. He slumped into a chair. He hadn't been as prepared to see her as he'd thought he was. His emotions had been on an out-of-control roller-coaster ride since Justin had broken the news.

Justin hadn't been very tactful with the announcement either. He'd walked into Jeff's office and told him to stop what he was doing on the computer as he had news to tell him. It seemed that something had been bothering Lauren of late and when Justin had finally got the secret from his wife, he'd been floored.

Busy with his computer program, Jeff hadn't been paying much attention to Justin, until he'd simply blurted out that Tori was pregnant. Lauren had begged Justin to let Tori and Jeff handle it, but he hadn't agreed. So here he was, spilling the beans.

Once Jeff was certain he'd heard his twin correctly, it took him a second for the implications of Justin's words to sink in. Then he'd bolted upward.

He'd been ready to fly to Kansas City that minute, but Justin insisted that Jeff sit back down and cool off.

Jeff begrudgingly admitted it might be wise to have a breathing period.

After Jeff had gotten over his shock, he'd been furious. He had tried to get himself under control by doing some work, but he couldn't concentrate and ended up forming plan after plan. Then he'd made his move.

Unfortunately, things hadn't worked out as he'd hoped.

When had Tori become this stubborn? Had she always been this way? Long ago they'd discussed the possibility of this situation, had the Pill failed, or at least he thought they had. They'd agreed to marry if this rarity ever occurred.

No, he'd wanted to get married, he admitted to himself. Tori hadn't agreed or disagreed. She probably didn't even remember the conversation. Had he even voiced it? Stress had him sighing. He didn't remember.

Admittedly, pregnancy suited her. She had that womanly glow he'd seen on Lauren, only Tori wore it differently. Maybe because the baby was his. Maybe because *she* was his. When he'd leaned on her desk, her scent had permeated his senses and he'd found himself a bit shaken—he still wanted her badly. He hadn't been lying when he'd said he missed her.

He'd always found her an attractive, fascinating woman—had desired her from the very first moment he'd laid eyes on her. After the company Christmas party almost three years ago he hadn't wasted the opportunity to claim her. He'd pursued her, seduced her and found nirvana when he'd made love to her. Sex wasn't necessarily a spiritual experience, but with Tori it was different. He'd never quite put his finger on why, only that she was somehow a part of him, one he hadn't planned to let go.

Jeff finished his beer, tossed the bottle into the trash can and chastised himself. He was pathetic. As Tori had said, maybe he did only care about how her body had made his feel. Wasn't he just thinking about that?

"So what are you going to do?" Clint asked, his voice permeating Jeff's thoughts.

Jeff wished he could give his friend an answer to that question. "I have no idea. What do you do when someone refuses to marry you? As she so aptly snapped at me, these aren't caveman days. I'd get arrested if I tossed her over my shoulder and carried her off."

"True," Clint agreed. "Do you love her?"

Jeff frowned. "She asked me that same question."

Clint stared at his friend and shook his head. "Jeff, women don't have to get married just because they're pregnant. Why do you want to marry her? That's an important question. How do you feel?"

Jeff honestly didn't know. Sure, he had feelings, but Tori had said those weren't enough. She was convinced she was right, and Jeff hadn't known Tori to be wrong very often. Maybe people in love were like computers needing more memory—some just weren't built to handle it and you had to get a new model. The thought that he possibly couldn't fall in love smarted. He'd never considered himself inadequate before, but this was definitely an area in which he was lacking.

"You are clueless when it comes to this stuff, aren't you?" Clint asked.

"What do you mean by that?" Jeff snapped.

"Nothing," Clint said, changing the subject. "So when are you returning to St. Louis?"

"I have to be there tomorrow night no matter what. My parents' anniversary is just around the corner and my brothers and I doing a huge family dinner at six o'clock to celebrate. I guess I've got a present for my mom now. Surprise, Mom! I'm going to give you another grandchild."

"You could always set your mother on Tori. Rose Wright is a dynamo." Clint chuckled, and although it really wasn't funny, Jeff did agree with Clint's assessment.

Jeff's mother, barely five feet tall, had raised three boys and was not afraid to speak her mind. The only positive in the entire Tori situation was that Justin had agreed to keep silent and allow Jeff to tell their mom about the baby himself. "I wouldn't subject anyone— much less Tori—to an inquisition by my mother. Those are lethal."

"Still, you know your mom. The moment you tell her about the baby she'll probably do it anyway. Your mother is very family-oriented, which is why she's always dragging your family to Branson, Missouri, for Christmas with your dad's parents. You know your mom isn't going to take the news that you fathered a baby sitting down."

"Probably not," Jeff agreed. "Although she always did want a lot of grandchildren."

"Ha," Clint said. "She didn't mean this way."

"Yeah," Jeff said. His mother was going to be extremely disappointed in him—even more so when she discovered he wasn't getting married.

"Perhaps I should talk to Tori?" Clint offered. "We always got along when I worked at the company. I do have to pop by tomorrow morning and see her anyway about those publicity brochures I'm doing for you."

"No!" The word shot forth from Jeff's lips faster than a bullet. "While I appreciate the offer, I'll handle this. I know her best, or at least I thought I did." He thought for a moment. "She's stubborn, but I'm sure I can persuade her to come around. Hopefully."

"She's a woman. She's not going to persuade easily. I mean, she's probably looking at what she's giving up if she marries you."

"Why does everyone think marrying me would be so bad?" Jeff asked. "Earlier you said I was clueless."

Clint gazed at his friend as though he were. "She's a woman. She wants it all," Clint told him. "You have to give her that."

Jeff frowned. He could do many impossible things, but saying he loved her when he wasn't sure how he felt just to get her to marry him was not one of them.

"I'll work this out," Jeff said.

"For your sake, I hope so. I wish you luck," Clint said. He raised his beer bottle in a salute.

"Thanks," Jeff said. He clenched and unclenched his fist, trying and failing to release some stress. Unlike a computer problem, he couldn't just reload the program and start over. He couldn't recover the data and move on. No, he had to face it, the situation with Tori was pretty dire and, for once, there might not be an answer. He hated to think that way. There was always a solution.

"So, do you want to go grab some dinner?" Clint asked. "I'm meeting up with some vendors I know. You're welcome to come along."

"No, thanks," Jeff said, mulling over how much he'd screwed up. He was about to be a father and the mother of his child wanted him as far away from her as possible. No matter what, Jeff planned to be a good dad. He wanted to be there as his child grew up the way his father had been for him. An idea began to take root in the back of his brain. Like a lightbulb, the thought became brighter and brighter and Jeff relaxed as an idea of what he could do started to form. "I'll just order room service and eat in."

He had plans to make.

JEFF ARRIVED AT TORI'S office the next morning at 10:00 a.m. The report she'd been about to e-mail to Jared could wait. Feminine pride dictated that Tori at least finger comb her hair before their meeting, but instead of cooperating, stress had left her brown locks lifeless. She tucked the offending pieces behind her ears and resolved to make this visit quick. They could work out all the visitation and support details later, after the baby's birth.

She pressed the intercom button on her phone. "Send him in," she told Darci.

It took only seconds for Jeff to arrive. He was again dressed in a casual polo shirt and pressed chinos, only the colors were different; he filled the doorway as he stepped through.

"Hello, Tori," he said, his gaze scrutinizing her appearance. "I hope you got some rest last night."

Tori swallowed, gathered her composure and wished his presence would someday stop affecting her. While she had a solid backbone, his innate maleness still sidetracked her, as it had from the beginning. She'd spent a restless night tossing and turning, her dreams filled with baby bootees and Jeff Wright.

She kept her voice deliberately neutral and polite. "Hi, Jeff. I'm fine. Thanks for asking." She took a deep breath and dug in. "You know, you really didn't have to come by today."

Those fathomless green eyes didn't blink as they assessed her. "I told you before I left I would be here and I keep my promises, Tori. I always have."

He had, and a tinge of guilt stole over her. Unfortunately, he'd never promised to love her. "I know you have, but that doesn't mean I'm going to change my mind. We're better as friends, Jeff. Let's leave everything that way and time will give us the perspective to work things out."

"Maybe you're right."

Tori stared at him. That was it? He was rolling over? She stole a glance at him. He remained standing, rubbing an invisible spot on his chin with his right forefinger. Then he moved a chair and placed it closer to her desk. He sat, bringing himself to her eye level. "After I returned to my hotel, I realized that I should have been more sensitive to your feelings. I've been selfish. Call it my own foolish male pride. I heard I'm about to be a father from my brother, who badgered it out of his wife. Not from you. That hurt."

"I'm sorry," she said, angry at herself for not telling him at the beginning.

"Anyhow, the more I thought about the situation, the more I wanted to apologize if any of my behavior yesterday was inappropriate. I don't want to fight with you, Tori, but you have to understand that you can't shut me out."

She stared at Jeff, but she couldn't sense if his neutral facade was only a ploy. He seemed genuine. She swallowed. "I don't want to shut you out and I won't, but you and I need to be up front that we have no future.

Not as a couple. As parents, well, that's coming regardless. The rest, including how we're going to handle raising the baby, I'd rather work out later when I've thought things through more. I still have many personal decisions to make, like where I want to live."

"As much as I'd like to give you that time, later is here," Jeff said. "You've never met my mother. The child you carry is her grandchild. She's all about family and family values. Once she finds out you're pregnant, everything will be a whole lot more complicated. One, I'm going to disappoint her terribly by not having been married first. I can't fix that, but I'd like to at least know where all the rest stands. I'd like to be a father to our baby starting today. That's why we have to discuss a lot of these things now."

"We'll just have to make your mother understand that times have changed," Tori said. "You can be involved, but I'm not marrying you."

"You said that and I got it," Jeff said, pausing for a second. "And for the final time, I think that you and I can make this work. You mean more to me than anyone else."

She could hear the sincerity in his voice but his declaration came too late and fell too short. He still hadn't said the words she really wanted to hear—"I love you." Not "more to me than anyone else."

"Jeff, I'm sorry. Maybe it would be better if we handled things through lawyers so we can keep our emotions out of creating the parenting plan."

Jeff's expression didn't change, and the croissant she'd eaten for breakfast churned in her stomach. "I'd rather not," he said, his voice tired. "We should both be able to be adult about this. I'm willing to try if you are."

Despite her attempts to stay in control, her voice escalated slightly. "I'm trying. Can't you see I'm trying?"

"I wish I could believe that," he said. "I really do. But you've kept me in the dark since the beginning, something you promised me you'd never do if this ever happened. We both knew abstinence is the only way to be sure and we weren't having that." He gave a harsh laugh. "I trusted you. I feel as if you've had no respect for my feelings. It's like you assume I don't have any. Well, I do."

As Jeff drew a hand through his red hair, Tori wished she'd had the foresight to grab some bottled water before he'd arrived. Anything to help her composure, anything to keep her from screaming in frustration. He might have feelings, but they weren't the ones she wanted him to have. She could ask him right now if he loved her and the answer would be no.

She stood up, the chair scooting erratically out from underneath her. Chin held defiant, she swept by him toward the louvered doors that hid her mini-refrigerator.

Strong fingers reached out, snared her wrist and stopped her flight. She whirled around, her body shocked by the dangerous heat generated by his touch. Tori jerked her hand back and he let her wrist go, breaking the electric current traveling between them. She clenched her fists. Even standing over him didn't give her any advantage. This man was her downfall.

"You are so stubborn. It's normally one of the things I adore about you, except now. Can't you see what's best for the baby is for us to work together?" he asked.

Tori paled slightly. "I am doing what's best for the baby. Our baby deserves a family where his or her parents love each other deeply, as Hailey has with Justin and Lauren. When you find your perfect partner, I'll be thrilled. When I find mine, we'll all be happy. And our child will have more people in his life who love him."

Jeff stood, his long body uncoiling as he rose from the chair. Tori trembled slightly. She'd loved this man, held him in her arms. She'd made love to him until both of them had drifted into a contented and satiated sleep. She'd ached for him and she'd wanted nothing more than to spend the rest of her life by his side. She'd loved him, but he hadn't reciprocated—he'd told her the relationship was perfect as it was.

Now, he'd offered her marriage, but for all the wrong reasons. He didn't love her. She doubted he ever would.

"So that's really what you want? Love?"

He said it like he didn't believe the answer could be so simple or inane.

"Yes," she said, her body trembling. "What we had was some good times. Lust. Chemistry. We connect on that level. Let's do ourselves a favor and try not to make what we shared into something more. You made it clear long ago that you were comfortable with the way our relationship was. And it rings hollow for you to say otherwise now that the circumstances have changed. You're not a settle-down family-man type."

He stared at her for a moment, almost as if seeing her for the first time. "I'm sorry you think that."

"I'm sorry, too," she admitted. "That's why you and I getting married would not solve our problems and would only make them worse. And I'm not having our child grow up in a family where the parents are playing house. I want it all."

"Everyone deserves that," he said.

"I think so." She turned away from him. She really wanted a drink of water and opened the doors to the cabinet that held the mini-refrigerator.

"I didn't intend to make things between us worse or

upset you. I have to be in St. Louis for my parents' anniversary tonight. How about we continue this later? Minus the discussions about us. The past is, well, past, I guess."

She grabbed a bottle of water. "Jeff, I just want to be left alone for a while." She did. This was a huge life change. She'd wanted her part settled—housing, childcare, hospital—before dealing with Jeff. When he attacked a problem, he could be like a bulldozer.

"I can't do that," Jeff said. His voice was quiet. "I'm sorry, Tori, but leaving you alone is the one thing I can't do."

The door clicked open and then shut behind him; Tori's shoulders slumped in defeat as she heard him leave. She returned to her chair and took a long drink.

She'd made such a mess of things. She patted her stomach. "It'll be okay, little one. It'll be okay."

She only wished she could believe.

JEFF STEPPED INTO the hallway and breezed past Darci. Within minutes, he was in the parking lot starting his rental car. He hadn't wanted to stress Tori, but he had finally got to the heart of the matter, which, ironically, was just that—Tori's heart.

She loved him. Or at least she had. He suddenly realized that he'd probably broken her heart when he'd made it clear he considered their relationship was perfect as it was. It *had* been perfect. But now he could understand how that had affected her. It had crushed her dreams. When you love someone, you want to be with that person for all the little things. Just being compatible in bed isn't enough.

And Jeff wasn't like those guys who said they loved

you when they really didn't. Except for his family, he'd never told anyone those words. He also hadn't wanted to be like Tori's ex, saying things he didn't mean and then breaking her heart. So Jeff had opted for casual. He hadn't let himself care deeply for her, erring on the side of caution, having seen what his brothers had gone through post breakup. Practical Jeff knew it was better to install a virus program before you needed it than to try to repair the damage later. Better to be safe than let love destroy you. While he wasn't sure he loved Tori in that romantic, end-all, be-all way, he did know one thing—for his sake and the baby's sake, he had to get her back.

Chapter Six

Jeff's parents' thirty-eighth anniversary dinner occurred at Henrietta's Restaurant in St. Louis. Known for impeccable service and phenomenal food, Henrietta's was the perfect place for the Wright family to celebrate the occasion.

Of course, Jeff had dressed up—coat and tie were required at Henrietta's. He tugged on his tie and tried to loosen the offending pin-striped version his mother had given him last Christmas. He hated ties, but twice a year he made the sacrifice—for her anniversary and her birthday. The two dinners were a tradition the boys had started after their company had first turned a profit. Since then, the family gatherings had grown from five attendees to seven. The only one without a spouse was Jeff, a fact that was bugging him today.

It was also a fact his mother had mentioned in passing more than once and the appetizers hadn't even arrived. Now that Jared and Justin were wed, Rose Wright's latest bent was to see Jeff head down the aisle. Tonight could be a long night, especially when he announced his news and what he had planned.

Jeff reached forward and swirled his glass of wine,

although he wasn't really interested in the merlot. He'd have only one drink all evening, raising his glass for various toasts. Tori loved wine. The night they'd first gotten together she'd imbibed way too much. She'd been upset about an ex, and Jeff had taken her up to her hotel room and tried to sober her up with black coffee.

He couldn't remember if she'd pounced on him or vice versa. It didn't really matter. The other guy was out of the picture, and Jeff had been waiting for his chance. He sighed, the sound lost in the noise of the animated crowd. Ever since walking out of Tori's office this morning, he'd been analyzing his relationship with her—from the moment they'd first met to the moment he'd left her today and all points in between.

His mother laughed at something and Jeff glanced at her. His mom would have about three glasses of wine during the course of the evening, each one loosening her tongue.

He didn't want to tell her he'd asked Tori to marry him and that she'd said no. The thought still rattled him. He'd never failed so badly at something this important before.

The entire conversation kept replaying in his mind like a bad movie that was on every channel. No matter how many times he pressed the remote, the picture never changed.

He wouldn't have gone to Kansas City if he didn't care. He wouldn't have asked her to marry him—for she was right, a man didn't have to do that these days. He liked being with her. She was fun, intelligent. They could hold animated conversations. He loved kissing her and tumbling her into bed. Marriage wouldn't be simply "playing house," as she'd called it.

But the L-word... He had to admit he understood what she meant by refusing to settle down without it. Jared's wife had been the same way.

Jeff set his wineglass down and surveyed his family. His parents were celebrating almost forty years of marriage. Sure, they bickered now and then, but you could see the love in their eyes whenever they looked at each other. Jeff didn't know if his sixty-something parents did anything in the bedroom besides sleep, but he did know they'd be lost without each other.

Jared felt the same way about his wife, and while Jeff had grown up sharing a bedroom with Justin and the twins had a deep bond, if Justin ever had to choose between Jeff and Lauren, he'd choose his wife.

And he should, Jeff told himself. Justin was gaga over Lauren. Two years ago, Jeff had been instrumental in giving his brother a kick in the pants when Justin had almost screwed up his chance to be with her. Jeff had known his brother was in love with Lauren when Justin nursed her through the flu. He'd waited on Lauren hand and foot, bringing her silly gifts to make her happy.

Jeff sipped his wine. Would he do that for Tori? He'd never known her to be sick. If she were, being as independent as she was, she probably wouldn't tell him. She hadn't told him she was on antibiotics the weekend she'd conceived.

Their relationship wasn't like that. Small details had always been ignored.

Jeff winced. He'd been an idiot. A first-class one by the looks of it. Not only did Tori not tell him when she was sick, she didn't even keep a toothbrush at his place. What did that say about their ability to get married? When she took off that last Sunday they were together, she'd scoured the place of her presence in five minutes or less.

Oh, he had little reminders of her. Long ago she'd given him a stuffed frog she'd named Prince that she'd created herself at one of those build-your-own-bear stores in the mall. She'd put a pith helmet on it and brought it to him.

Aware of his love for sports cars, she'd given him an assortment of Hot Wheels cars, the two-inch-long kind that ran on racetracks. Over the first few months they'd dated, she'd bought him models of classic sports cars, a Corvette, a Porsche, a Ferrari and a… His mind blanked. He wasn't sure what they all were, but he had about twelve altogether. When she'd stopped adding to the collection, he'd simply forgotten about them. They sat on top of a shelf, all in a row. He'd planned on giving them to Jared's son when he was older and could make use of them.

Now Jeff could see the cars for what they were— Tori's attempt to bring some normalcy to the relationship. People who cared for each other bought each other gifts and did little things for each other, just because. Jeff had got too comfortable too fast with Tori. He listened. He gave her endless orgasms. But he'd forgotten to woo her, forgotten the importance of the grand gesture.

Wooing had never been important to Jeff before. His work claimed his time and no woman had ever held his interest long enough for him to even think about the small details, such as remembering what they liked to eat for dinner. But Tori had had him from the get-go. She'd stolen his attention from the minute he'd met her. For six years he'd been on the periphery, a moth flitting around a flame.

And then, after he'd gotten together with her and survived the rough spots at the beginning, he'd relaxed and gone back to the casual attitude by which he lived his life. Case closed. He had her. He'd won. She was with him and he was happy. All was well. Never once had he realized anything was amiss and never once had she told him. Oh, she'd told him she wanted more, but when he'd rejected that and she hadn't left, he'd made the dumb-male assumption that everything was A-okay. He'd been so content that he'd never noticed the fire slowly dying in her eyes.

"Earth to Jeff," Justin said, waving a fork in the air. "You planning on adding to this conversation or staring at your drink all night?"

Absorbed in his own thoughts, Jeff had no idea what they'd been talking about or if it involved him. "I thought zoning out was a good way to stay out of trouble," he said, grinning.

"Ha," Jared said, not buying it.

"They were telling me you aren't seeing Tori anymore," his mother said, her gaze locked on to Jeff's like a homing beacon. Jeff grimaced. So they *had* been discussing him. "What happened to this one? She must have had potential if she put up with your nonsense for as long as she did. For two years I've waited to meet her and now she's gone? What did you do this time?"

Great, Jeff thought. While he'd been lost in his thoughts, his brothers had tried—and failed—to divert their mother's attention from his love life. Next time he'd pay better attention to the conversation.

"She dumped me, Mom," Jeff said, which wasn't necessarily a lie. Tori had sent him an e-mail. She'd told him to his face. She'd refused to marry him. She'd asked him to leave.

"So what if she dumped you?" his mom arched a dark eyebrow, indicating she expected more from him. That was the thing about Rose Wright. She wasn't known to give up easily. "How do *you* feel about that?"

"I'm dealing with it," Jeff said. "Who am I to argue if she wants to move on with her life? We're planning on being friends and, since she still works for the company, I'll see her again soon."

Justin choked on a sip of water and Lauren patted him on the back. Jeff glared at his twin.

"When?" his mother asked.

"When I go to Kansas City," Jeff said. "She moved there to take a job heading up our West Coast office."

"So you gave up on her because of distance?"

"No. She's changed."

"You always have an excuse. Family's just not important to you," Rose scoffed. Jeff knew she was referring to the many times he'd managed to be out of town for extended family functions that he deemed silly, such as some third cousin's birthday party or something. His mother wasn't talking about immediate family; he was always there for those events.

She shot him a hard look. "If you don't get off your behind, you'll be an old man with only that horrid cat to keep you warm at night."

"Buddy is not a horrid cat," Jeff corrected. "He just has an alley-cat temperament that occasionally causes him to scratch things."

"At least he's not out carousing," Rose snapped.

"I'm not either," Jeff said, grateful to see the appetizers arrive.

"You're not out at all," she said, refusing to let the subject go. His mother could take any argument and beat it to death. "How are you going to find a nice girl if you keep your nose pressed against the computer screen? You need to be out there."

"What, barhopping?" Jeff said.

She narrowed her eyes, green like Jeff's. "Don't try to trip me up. You know exactly what I mean. You keep letting all the good ones get away."

"Jeff really liked Tori," Justin inserted smoothly, giving his brother a smile that made Jeff instantly tense. "He did just go see her. Maybe he's trying to win her back."

"That would be a start," Rose snapped.

"I'm sure he's done more than start," Justin continued. "That's what you were doing, right?"

"What else could it be?" Jeff said, sending his brother one of those "if looks could kill" warning glances.

"I don't know," Justin needled. "Why don't you tell us what else it could be?"

"Anything would be an improvement over the current situation," Rose said. She glanced at her sons. "Is there more you need to tell me?" his mother asked, her hand hovering over the marinara sauce, the toasted ravioli in her fingers just waiting to be dipped. "Jeff?"

"Oh, there is," Justin promised.

Lauren appeared stricken while everyone else was merely curious, having no clue where this conversation was going. As for Jeff, he wanted to leap across the table and punch the smug expression off his brother's face. This had to be payback for some childhood prank, long forgotten on his part.

But maybe now *would* be a good time to spill his news, and the idea he'd arrived at last night when he'd been searching for a sliver of hope—anything to convince Tori to marry him.

"Actually, there is more," Jeff admitted. He drained the wineglass in front of him. "I guess this is as good a place as any to announce it, but I've decided that my department would be better served from the Kansas City office. Since, essentially, I am my own department, I'm relocating."

"You're what?" Surprised, Justin dropped the escargot he'd been holding and it landed with a splat in the butter dish. Everyone else stared.

"Relocating in early August," Jeff said. *Ha. Take that, brother dear.* "I've decided to sell the condo and buy a house. The cost of living's a little cheaper on the other side of the state, and I want to concentrate less on responding and more on preventative measures and systems design, as we'd always planned on me doing."

"You are just making this up on the fly," Justin accused. "Have you even thought this through?"

Jared turned his head as if watching a tennis match.

"Honey," Lauren said, placing a pacifying hand on Justin's arm.

"I haven't worked out every detail," Jeff admitted, staring his brother down. "But I mean every word of it."

"You're moving?" Jeff's mother was stunned. Jeff's dad, Victor, appeared surprised as well. "I like having all my sons near me."

"Yeah, but I want to be near my son. Or daughter," Jeff said. Only a moment passed before everyone but Lauren and Justin gasped.

"What?" This from his father and Jared.

Jeff wasn't sure who'd voiced the question first and he took a deep breath. "Tori is pregnant. I've asked her to marry me. Several times."

"You're getting married?" His mother seemed confused yet hopeful.

"No, I'm not getting married," Jeff said. "Tori hasn't accepted my proposal. If I want to be a part of her life—and my child's—I'm going to have to move to Kansas City."

"Well, I'll be," Justin said. He leaned back in his chair, surprised but impressed. "I didn't think you'd have it in you."

"Neither did I," Jeff admitted. "But a man has to do everything he can to right the situation."

"You're just lucky we're a family-owned company and that you can make spontaneous decisions like this," Jared said, still processing everything as he ate a bite of toasted ravioli.

"You're just lucky I'm working for you at all," Jeff said, playing his ace in the hole. "I'd be pretty sought after if I were a free agent, and you know it."

"Touché," Justin said, raising his wineglass. Besides being their brother and partner, Jeff was a stalwart of the organization. Many of the software programs he'd designed had got the company on its feet.

"Boys," their mother inserted, regaining control of the conversation. "I'm not having any more work talk at the table. Not on my anniversary." She turned to Jeff, the ravioli she'd been about to eat resting ready on her plate. "You're going to try to get Tori to marry you, aren't you?"

"Absolutely," Jeff said. While Tori might not yet be agreeable, he planned to win her back. Winning her the first time had taken tenacity and guts. This second time would be different, and harder.

"And do you love her?" his mother asked.

"I don't love her in the way she wants me to love her," Jeff said honestly. "But I do know that I want to be with her. I think about her a lot. I care about her and miss her. I want to be a partner to her in raising our child."

"Then you must start there," his mother said simply. She pushed her appetizer plate away and the waiter removed it. "Search your soul, and you'll know your path." With that, she lifted her fork and attacked her salad.

"That's it?" Justin suddenly asked as his mother dropped the topic. Justin's eyes twinkled, and Jeff could see his brother couldn't let this die yet. "You let him off with just a cheesy saying about knowing your path? After all the grief you gave me over the years, you aren't going to lay into him more?"

Rose swallowed her food. "Jeff's the thinker. You flew by the seat of your pants from one thing to the next. Jeff will do the right thing." She turned to her son, her expression dead serious. "Or else."

Chapter Seven

The day of Lisa Meyer's wedding to Mark Smith was perfect. The weather in St. Louis was surprisingly mild, a cold front having come through the day before the rehearsal, knocking the temperatures back into the low eighties. The sorority sisters were all ready.

"I feel as though I just did this," Cecile said, referring to her sister's wedding in June. Her strawberry-blond hair was swept up onto the top of her head, two curled tendrils framing her face.

Lisa was radiant in her white wedding gown, and Tori pushed away her envy. She was not going to be a sourpuss just because her best friends all seemed to have found the man of their dreams and she was still single. If tonight went well for Cecile, she could be the next one walking down the aisle.

"So is anyone besides me nervous?" Lisa suddenly asked.

"Me," Joann said. "My stomach is just bouncing. This baby has to be a girl. She's so different from the others."

"Four kids," Cecile said, her green eyes wide with unabashed awe.

"Yes, I know. I'm crazy. I told Kyle this was it."

The girls all laughed, knowing that Joann was quite happy and had willingly participated in the conception. Number four had been tried for and conceived; not a surprise as Tori's had been. Joann had just made her announcement yesterday.

"You doing okay, too, Tori?" Lisa asked.

"I'm hanging in there," Tori said. She was just starting to show, but the light pink sleeveless sheath dress hid it pretty well.

"Good," Lisa said, rising to her feet. "Because I do believe it's time. Everyone give me one last hug as a single woman."

The Roses got to their feet and had a touching group hug. The day flew by. Luke, Cecile's boyfriend, had shown up at the church and had commandeered Cecile, and Tori had made small talk with the groomsman who served as her date. He'd disappeared to join his friends soon after dinner ended, but Tori knew enough of the guests that the reception wasn't boring. In fact, it was about to get quite interesting, Tori thought, as Luke and Cecile slipped away.

Tori smiled to herself, her earlier pang of being the only single one left having come and gone. Another of her best friends was about to get her happy ending— that was the important thing. Her suspicions were confirmed when Tori saw Luke and Cecile leaving the koi pond area. Cecile's hair had completely fallen around her shoulders. Luke had his arm wrapped around her and Tori saw the flash of an engagement ring on her friend's finger as Cecile and Luke made a beeline for the house.

As she passed Tori, Cecile waved her goodbyes and mouthed the words, "You're next."

Then Cecile and Luke vanished, headed to a hotel suite, Tori surmised. That's where she'd go if she'd just said "yes" to the man of her dreams.

Tori watched the couple for a moment, happy for her friends. Mark and Lisa were in each other's arms, enjoying some time alone before another guest claimed their attention. Joann and Kyle were dancing, taking pleasure in a night *sans* children. Kyle's hand often strayed to his wife's stomach, cherishing the new life growing there.

Tori automatically reached to touch her own stomach, but she caught herself and took a sip of her cola instead.

On the night before their sorority initiation, the girls had camped out. Dreaming of the future, they'd predicted the order of their weddings. They'd also selected who'd be the maid of honor for whom. While the order hadn't gone as planned, the maid of honor duties had.

Lisa had stood next to Joann, who married right out of college. Today, Cecile had stood next to Lisa, and now that Cecile had just become engaged, Tori knew that, soon, Cecile would ask for her to be her maid of honor. And, of course, whenever Tori finally met her Mr. Right, Joann would stand next to Tori, making the circle complete.

Tori frowned as a thought unsettled her. Lisa had married superfast. If Cecile followed suit, Tori might be as big as a house by the wedding. A tear formed in her right eye and Tori quickly brushed it away. Dr. Hillyer had told her that she might experience unusual emotions because of her hormones. That had to be why she was so teary-eyed now. So what if she was pregnant? No way would she miss Cecile's wedding. Cecile was probably the type to take things slow anyway. Tori was due in December. Cecile had always said she wanted a June wedding. There would be plenty of time for both Tori and Joann—who was due in March—to get back in shape before then.

Tori took comfort in having such good friends. She stepped forward, but stopped when a hand firmly grabbed her arm. Her cola sloshed, barely missing her dress as she jumped backwards and held the glass straight out. Why, she ought to give the person a tongue-lashing for scaring her like this….

She turned. "Hi, Tori," Jeff said. "I thought it might be time we talked."

"Jeff! What are you doing here?" Tori's hand shook, and Jeff took the glass she was holding. He was dressed impeccably: white broadcloth shirt, pressed pants and a tie. As if he knew he was heading to a wedding reception. But she hadn't seen him at dinner.

"I came to find you," he said. "I figured this would be as good a place as any for us to connect."

"Lauren." Tori understood. Since she'd been in St. Louis, Tori had had a little time to run by Lauren's and see both her and Hailey before the rehearsal dinner. "She's always telling you what she shouldn't."

"Not everything. It took me a while to figure out where the reception was and figure out exactly when to arrive."

"You crashed?" Tori stared at him in shock. Never in a million years would she have ever believed Jeff capable of such action.

"I crashed," he admitted. "But since I came after dinner, I figured it wouldn't matter too much. Besides, I'm not here to eat or drink. I wanted to see you so we could talk."

"There's no need to talk. Nothing's going on," Tori said.

He tucked a strand of her hair behind her ear, the gesture intimate. Her body heated. "Maybe not on your end, but there are things on mine."

At that moment Lisa and Mark came over. "Hey Tori. Jeff. I didn't know you were coming." Lisa glanced at Tori, who shrugged.

"Last-minute change of plans," Tori said.

"Congratulations to both of you," Jeff said. He reached forward and shook Mark's hand.

"Thanks," Mark replied.

"Will you be here tomorrow afternoon for lunch?" Lisa asked, her attention on Tori.

"Yes. I'm not leaving until Monday night. I've got meetings here Monday morning."

"Then I'll see you tomorrow." Lisa drew Tori into a hug and whispered in her ear, "You okay?"

She'd probably never be okay again. "I'm fine," Tori lied. "I'll fill you in tomorrow."

"I want to know everything," Lisa whispered. "And I mean *everything*."

"And I'll tell you," Tori said. The two women broke apart and, within seconds, Tori and Jeff were alone.

"Let's not talk here," Jeff said. "Come on. Go get your stuff."

"I'm not leaving with you," Tori said, the volume of her voice notching up slightly. Pregnancy had messed with her hormones and, frankly, she knew she wasn't safe around Jeff. Joann had coined the phrase "happy hormones," referring to that time during pregnancy when a woman was quite, er, wanton and insatiable. Some women in the office had confided that they'd never had happy hormones, but Tori simply looked at Jeff and hers kicked in. If she left with him, she knew she'd cave and do things she'd enjoy but regret later.

"So you want to talk here then?" Jeff asked. Tori glanced around. Already a few people were staring. "Do you hate me that much that you don't even trust me anymore?"

She frowned as his words struck home. "I don't hate you. And I do trust you," she said—both statements were true.

"Then let's take this back to my place," he said, reaching to cup her elbow.

Tori shook her head, her hair swishing around her chin. Already his touch was sending waves of desire through her. "No."

Jeff let go and took a step back so he could better read her expression. "Why not?"

Didn't he understand? "We'll just end up in bed," Tori said. "That's where this relationship went wrong in the first place. We're all passion and no substance."

Jeff dropped his hands to his side. "Okay. We'll talk here. Is there somewhere more private?"

Tori stared at him. Once again he'd given in to what she'd asked. "Follow me." She led him to the bench by the koi pond. After sitting, she took off the two-inch strappy sandals that matched the pale-pink bridesmaid dress she wore. When she'd first seen the gown, Tori had loved it immediately. However, the shoes were another story. They were pure torture and she worried she'd have blisters.

"So what did you want to discuss?" she asked.

"I told my parents about the baby," Jeff said, settling down beside her.

Great. "How did your mom take it?"

"She wishes we were getting married."

"I can't," Tori said.

He shifted slightly. "I understand."

"Cecile's getting married. She and Luke just got engaged tonight. They seem really in love and happy. I can't simply marry you because I feel like life is starting to pass me by."

"Which is why you took the job and moved to Kansas City this past spring," Jeff said. "I get that now."

"Good." Tori leaned forward, watching a fish swim in the lighted pond as she tried to gather her thoughts. In business, she could hold a conversation with the best of them. This talk with Jeff was rattling her, making her feel as if she were trying to paddle upstream. Now instead of demanding, he was being extremely civil, changing the rules of this "fight" again. However, maybe this was good. Maybe they could forge a truce.

"You and I were in a rut. I needed more from our relationship, but you didn't love me," she said.

He sat there, not denying it and she took his silence as acquiescence. "Taking the KC job was an opportunity I couldn't pass up—the opportunity of a lifetime. At least I could have that."

"And I can't fault you for wanting to advance in your career," Jeff said. "You've done a great job, and Jared's raving about the work you're doing. Justin's even said good things, and you know what a tightwad he can be with everything from money to compliments."

"That's true. Lauren once confided she'd thought Justin was a scrooge when he questioned her decisions regarding the company Christmas party."

"He was used to beer and nachos, which was how

we'd done it in the beginning when we were broke and just starting out. Lauren wanted something formal. I really liked the party the way she did it. Especially afterward."

Tori blushed. "You did pursue me relentlessly," she said.

He nodded. "I had to. You'd stopped dating what's-his-name. It was my one and only chance before you inevitably met someone else. As it was, you went back to him."

"You confused me," Tori admitted, feeling a bit more at ease with the conversation now. "You always have. We've never had many expectations. You made it clear."

She could remember the day vividly: Jeff had been pressing buttons on the remote, choosing another movie channel. She'd asked him where he thought their relationship was headed, and he'd fallen silent until he'd finally said, "I like things the way they are." He'd then faced her. "Don't get me wrong. You know how much I care about you, but I'm not ready to settle down. I don't have long-term relationships. No one can handle my work schedule. You've outlasted everyone else in my life."

"Because I don't push too hard," she'd said. "I don't make demands."

"And I like that about you," he'd replied, but the words hadn't warmed her. "You aren't manipulative or clingy. You don't have a stopwatch demanding that I marry you or else you're leaving me. Any woman who did that would be gone within minutes. I'm a man who needs his space and his freedom."

"You like everything in its place," Tori had told him. She knew Jeff compartmentalized all the details of his life, as if every person had his or her own little box and Jeff took a box out and played with it once in a while.

Jeff hadn't denied her words. "It's like being together is our own mini-escape," he'd said, giving her the reasons why he refused to want anything else. "You know I live my life on call. The phone rings constantly. My pager beeps. If there's a crisis, I can be there within minutes. But everyone knows that Saturday nights belong just to us. No one phones. No one disturbs us. We focus just on us and being together. It's ideal."

But it hadn't been, at least not for her. One night of attention was not enough.

Tori refocused on the situation at hand. Jeff sat beside her on a bench in a quiet part of Mark's parents' backyard.

"I can't go back to that life with you," she finally said. "All we did was sit, watch movies, eat dinner and have sex. There's no use in dragging ourselves through this again. We need to move forward."

"I agree, although I liked those evenings. You know my ideal night is kicking back with a brew and watching television. Having you there was a delightful bonus and I cherished those times. I don't want to be a part of some stupid social scene where everyone plasters on fake smiles. Attending family events drives me nuts and I try to avoid them at all costs. Ask Justin. He'll tell you that I always win the most-creative-excuse award."

She knew all this. She also knew Jeff didn't play traditional dating games. *That meant*—she paused—*he had come and found her tonight.*

"I think we can work out some sort of friendship," she said. "I'm sorry if I said you wouldn't be good father material—I was out of line. I'm sure you'll love the baby." A stab of bitterness pierced her. He would love his child, just not her.

"When I babysat Hailey the other day, we had a great time," Jeff said, missing her discomfort.

"But, she's not yours. You don't see her when she shrieks or cries. You don't often get to see her at her worst." Tori wasn't convinced.

"That still doesn't mean I won't make a good father," Jeff said. "I mean, it's not something you learn in school but how hard can it be? I'd like to think that I could be a little more involved than just getting you pregnant then running."

"But you do run. You're constantly on the road. Could you give that up?"

"Actually, I have." He said it with such conviction that Tori did a double-take.

"What do you mean by that?"

"Even though other fathers travel constantly and E.R. doctors have twelve-hour shifts and are successful parents, I knew you needed more from me. So I did a little rearranging."

Tori didn't get what he meant and found herself on guard. Jeff was looking at her like the cat that swallowed the cream. "Okay," she said slowly.

"You know my goal has always been to get to the point in the company where I could focus less on being a first-responder and troubleshooter. I want to work more on preventative measures and systems design. The best way for me to do that would be to do what you did."

Dread stole over her. He wouldn't. He couldn't. "And what's that?" she asked, steeling herself for the answer.

"I want to be a part of my child's life. I can't do that living in St. Louis. Starting Monday, I'm relocating my division to Kansas City. You and I, Tori, are about to be partners again."

Chapter Eight

He'd trapped her. Tori stared at him, not bothering to hide her disbelief. She lashed out with the first thing she could think of. "Kansas City is *my* office. I should have been consulted on this," she accused.

"It wasn't your decision to make," Jeff said. "Jared's the company president. I proposed the idea and he agreed. Jared wouldn't send me here if it was going to cost Wright Solutions money."

Her panic increased. Once she would have loved this, like back when she'd believed he might come to love her. Now circumstances had changed. The baby already had her tied to Jeff, and now he'd be back in the office. Right down the hall, always underfoot. How was she supposed to move on with her life? The only way would be to give up her job. And who would hire a pregnant woman at her high salary, knowing that she would be taking maternity leave? She was stuck.

"It's not going to be that bad," Jeff said.

"Yes, it is. You didn't even ask me my opinion. This is a done deal."

"Yes." His one word said it all.

"You didn't tell me." Her voice dropped as she finally understood.

"No. I didn't tell you," Jeff said. "And before you think I did this to spite you for keeping your news secret or for dumping me and moving across the state, let me assure you that's hardly my reason. I don't want to be your enemy, Tori. You're carrying my child and I want to be a part of my son or daughter's life. I am going to be there for our baby—and you—and I can't do that if I live on the other side of the state. I've done enough traveling. I want stability. I want what's best for everyone, including you. That means I need to move."

Tears welled up in Tori's eyes. "But you *aren't* what's best for me," she said, blurting out the words.

Jeff was already on his feet, and he used his thumb and forefinger to lift her chin. "Yes, I am," he said simply. "I am what's best for you and you're what's best for me. And I'm going to prove it to you."

"You don't love me," she said. "I'm not marrying without love."

"Then I'll at least be in Kansas City to watch my child grow up. I'll be in the office if you and I need to talk about the baby's education, health, whatever. I'm not going to be a disappearing dad or a bad one," he insisted.

"I'll believe that when I see it," Tori said. She stood, feeling overwhelmed. "I really need to get back to the reception. People will miss me. I have a job to do."

To her surprise, he didn't protest. He rose to his feet. "Fine."

"You're coming with me?" she asked, surprised.

"That's the way to go home," he said. "I only came here to talk with you. Obviously my timing wasn't great, but I didn't want you to hear this from anyone else but me. Jared was planning on filling you in when you meet with him."

"Thank you," Tori said, respecting that decision. At least she wouldn't be blindsided when she met with Jared in two days. "I appreciate that."

"Tori," Jeff said.

He stood there in the glow of the koi pond and Tori's heart broke a little. He was so handsome and beautiful. But she wanted the emotion, not just what was on the surface. "What?" she asked.

"I'm serious. I want us to work this out." He appeared so sincere, but she knew that without love nothing mattered.

"We can't," she said. "There is no us anymore. That's just the way it's going to have to be."

He nodded. "Okay, then. I'll see you later." He followed her down the path, parting ways with her once they returned to the reception. She watched him go.

"Is he leaving?" Joann had moved to her side.

"Yes," Tori said. "I told him there's not going to be a round two."

"That's what he came for?"

"He also wanted to tell me he was moving to Kansas City. He's relocating. He's going to be working out of my office. Well, my office building."

"Oh," Joann said.

"'Oh' is right," Tori replied. "Joann, I moved to get away from him. Now he'll be around the corner, where I can run into him constantly, not just in the office but in town, too. That's going to make finding a new man difficult. It'll be like Big Brother watching."

"Jeff *is* the baby's father," Joann pointed out.

"That doesn't mean he has the right to interfere with *my* life," Tori replied sharply.

"No," Joann said. "I agree with you there. But he's moving to be close to you and the baby. He wants to be a father. You ought to give him credit. A lot of men wouldn't do that."

Tori thought for a moment. "True," she admitted.

"So give him a chance to be a dad. No one's saying you have to fall in love with him, take him back or give up on finding your perfect match. At least be his friend and let him be a father."

Tori watched as Kyle approached in the distance. The reception was winding down and she would be spending the night upstairs in one of the Smith family's guest bedrooms. She couldn't wait to find some time to herself to relax, even for a minute.

"Just hang in there," Joann said as her husband joined them.

"I'll try," Tori said. At this point, what else could she do?

JEFF STARTED his home search on Monday, two days after seeing Tori at the wedding reception. He hadn't been surprised that she'd been so ticked. He knew he'd surprised her. Unless she chose to find another job, Tori would have to get used to having him around. Jeff sighed. He'd gambled and won the battle. But as for winning the war? Jeff had no illusions that he was anywhere close to doing that. He'd have to do what Lauren and his mother suggested—woo her.

So that's what he planned to do, starting with finding the perfect house. Something not too ostentatious. Something with three bedrooms and a decent yard.

Since the Wright Solutions office was located in a suburb of Kansas City, the real estate agent had suggested nearby Blue Springs where the housing was a bit more reasonable. Driving through the area, Jeff had agreed. He wanted to live in a neighborhood where Tori would feel comfortable, and he knew her parents lived only ten miles south of the development.

His search was short-lived; he found what he was looking for in the third house, a one-and-a-half story, with a master-bedroom suite on the first floor. The twenty-year-old home boasted a three-car garage, vaulted ceilings, a fireplace and a huge kitchen that was perfect for cooking and entertaining. Better yet, it had a living room he could use as a home office, a large great room and even a hearth room, which created additional living space off the kitchen. The yard, too, was perfect: a spacious deck with a screened-in porch overlooking a landscaped lawn complete with mature trees.

The agent was more than happy to write up his offer. He'd hear back within twenty-four hours.

As he paced his hotel room, Jeff found himself getting nervous. He'd really liked the house and hoped that he could reach an agreement with the owners.

Of course, there would be an inspection, but Jeff had immediately had a good feeling about the house. Usually he didn't trust his intuition—he preferred hard facts—but this time he'd decided to go with this gut.

He also had a pretty good suspicion that Tori was going to like the house, which was one of the main reasons he wanted to purchase it. It had the same open feeling her apartment in St. Louis had had and enough space for them to escape each other when necessary. Of course, that was after he convinced her to at least move in with him. Okay, forgiving him came first, but at least one piece was in place, almost.

Jeff glanced at his watch. He still had plenty of time to do the next thing on his list. The car dealerships were open late tonight, so he headed down to the hotel lobby and had the valet bring around his car. His Corvette sports car gleamed and, after he climbed in, he ran his hand across the dashboard. He sighed, steeled himself and reminded himself that Tori was worth the sacrifice.

"JEFF WRIGHT IS here to see you."

"Now?" The word slipped out before Tori had a chance to catch it. Still pressing the intercom button, she said, "Send him in."

She released her finger and gave herself a quick appraisal. She'd begun to put on weight so was wearing one of her new maternity dresses today, a dark-blue dress with a small, white floral print. She wasn't really showing that much, but as her baby grew the dress would flatter her figure and stretch along with her stomach. She rose when he entered. "Jeff. I wasn't expecting you today. Jared said you'd start work tomorrow, on Wednesday. Today's Tuesday. Is something wrong?"

"Nope," he said, a grin creasing his face. He was dressed in a polo shirt and jeans. He still wore leather boat shoes, minus the socks. She swallowed. He looked great, confident. Unlike her, he was relaxed. Casual. She was wound like a spring, trying to figure out how she was going to put up with him in the office on a daily basis. Once that had been easy to do, back when they'd been seeing each other.

"So why are you here?" she asked, sitting down.

"I'm not trying to be rude. I just don't have time to socialize. I was in St. Louis all yesterday. I've got three reports to finish and I'm running behind."

"I'm not here to socialize, either," Jeff said. He leaned over, giving her a whiff of his aftershave as he dropped a piece of paper on her desk. She fought down her body's heated reaction, damn those happy hormones, and reached for the document. While he sat down in the chair on the other side of her desk, the distance didn't necessarily give her the chance to compose herself. He leaned back and stretched out his legs.

She stared at the real-estate flyer he'd given her. "What's this?"

"A house."

She frowned at him. "I can see that."

"Like it?" he asked, his expression curious.

She studied the paper for a minute and then pushed it toward him. "It's very nice, but I'm not in the market for a house yet. My lease isn't even up until next year."

Jeff looked like a child about to share a secret. "You might not be, but I am. Was. I bought it yesterday. I close at the end of the month."

Tori's jaw dropped. "So moving here isn't just some temporary whim. You've actually bought a house in Kansas City."

"Yeah, well, Blue Springs. It's a nice neighborhood. Established. I want our child to have a place to call home. I think you'll like it."

The flyer did make the house sound very appealing.

"You bought a house." Tori shrugged. "You're really going to be mowing the lawn and all that stuff. That seems so, well, not you."

He grinned, seeing through her deliberate nonchalance. "That was the old me. This is the new me. I've already listed my condo. The Realtor in St. Louis said it should sell fast. My area's the latest hot spot or something. So, like Jared told you, I'm here for the duration. I'll be in a hotel until I get possession. Unless you'd like to put me up."

His teasing was infectious and normally that smile charmed the pants off her. Today, she simply stared at him, her mouth hanging open as if she were trying to scream, but nothing came out. "I'm not putting you up," she managed.

Heck, the fact that she hadn't murdered him for transferring was about as much good as he was going to get. Old Jeff or new Jeff. "What is this with 'the new me'?" she asked, unable to help herself.

"I'm going to be a dad. I need to make some changes. You, for obvious reasons, aren't returning to St. Louis. I'm not being a geography-challenged parent. So out with the condo, in with the house. Like I said, I plan to win you back."

"I don't want you back," she said.

"So you say," Jeff said in an easygoing manner that irritated the hell out of her. It was as if he planned to waltz back into her life, turn it upside down and expect her to be happy about it.

Hardly.

"I've given you the office down the hall on the other side of the building." *As far from me as I could put you*, Tori thought.

"You gave me the conference room?" Jeff asked, eyebrow arched.

"As part-owner, you rate the space. The conference

room's now moving upstairs. You know Jared—he's great with logistics and floor layouts and he approved it. Your office furniture will be delivered first thing tomorrow morning. You can't do much until then because that's when I was expecting you."

"I know. I've thrown a wrench into everything." Jeff didn't seem the least bit apologetic. "Since I've ruined the day, why don't you throw in the towel and come with me to see the house. I got special permission to show it to you. The Realtor is meeting us there in an hour."

As curious as she was, she couldn't let Jeff suck her back in. "I have to work. I can't just blow off an afternoon. I have reports to do."

"Not right now," Jeff said. His grin expanded. "The boss says so."

Tori stared at him. "I guess you do outrank me." She didn't like that fact at all.

He nodded, the charm that used to entice her rolling off him like waves. "Yes, I do, and in this situation I'm going to pull ownership privileges. However, before you work yourself into a tizzy, let me assure you that I'm not going to be messing with any of your day-to-day operations or company decisions. I'm not here to supervise you, and I'm not going to let anyone come to me so they can go over your head or behind your back. You run the show. But I want you to see the house and to get you there I'm taking out every weapon I have."

"And you're not afraid to use them," Tori stated flatly, a little flattered that he was beginning to finally fight for her. Too bad it was too late. Although, if he changed, really changed, was it?

He smiled a mischievous smile—he knew he was

about to get what he wanted. "Nope, I'm not. I want you to see the house and to be on time we have to leave now. Shut down your computer and let's go."

Tori glanced at the work she had to do, hesitating. While leaving might temporarily throw her off schedule, there was nothing that really couldn't wait until tomorrow.

"This is where our child is going to be spending a lot of time. Don't you want to see it? Offer some critique?"

His words sealed it. She was curious about what Jeff had bought for himself and their child. Frankly, the fact that Jeff had bought a house intrigued her. Houses required yard work and maintenance, both of which he studiously avoided. That's why he'd owned a condo.

She logged off her computer and rose to her feet.

"I like the dress," Jeff said, his gaze roving over her. "It's new, isn't it?"

"Yes, and thanks," Tori said, finding herself touched that he'd noticed. Normally he was oblivious to her attire, at least he'd never commented on it.

Within minutes they were in the elevator heading to the lobby. As they stepped outside, Tori paused and scanned the parking lot. Jeff's black Corvette convertible, usually extremely visible, was nowhere in sight. Her brow creased. "Are we taking my car?"

"No," he said. He pulled a key fob from his pocket. "I'm parked right over here." He pressed a button and the lights flashed on a new green minivan.

Tori's mouth dropped open. "You bought a minivan?"

He nodded as he strode over toward it. "Yes. I wanted something with doors that open via remote control. Lauren has last year's model and she loves it. She says she can carry Hailey and has no problem getting in the car."

"You bought a minivan," Tori repeated, the shock of what he'd done still not quite sinking in. Had Jeff changed? The thought was unreal. "You loved that convertible."

"No, I didn't," Jeff said. "It was a car. Gets you from point A to point B. Sure, it got me there in style, but I'm going to be a father. I had to have a vehicle with room for a car seat. The guy at the dealership even taught me how to load one in properly and use the safety buckle. And this car has the highest safety ratings."

"I can't believe you did this," Tori said. It was as if she'd stepped into a parallel universe. Similar, yet strange. "You've relocated and you've bought a new minivan."

Jeff seemed inordinately pleased with himself. "With the move to Kansas City, I'm also scaling back my traveling exponentially. I've told Jared that I want to be completely deskbound by the time the baby is born. By January, I shouldn't be traveling at all, except for the rare day trip to St. Louis now and then. I'll be home in the evenings."

"I never would have imagined," Tori said. He was more organized and prepared for the baby than she was, which was pretty scary.

"Of course not," Jeff said as he helped Tori into the car. She inhaled the new-car scent. "I got the leather because it cleans easier than cloth."

"It's nice," Tori said. "But it's still a minivan."

"I know," he said. "But this was an easy sacrifice. When I asked you to marry me, Tori, I was very serious. Even though you said 'No,' I'm determined to be a part of our child's life. I also want to be a part of yours. I'm going to show you that I can be not just a good father but a great one. You may not believe me, but I'm going to prove it to you. Starting today. Let's take a drive and see the house."

The house was beautiful, and Tori instantly fell in love with its spaciousness and location. Jeff had chosen well, she thought as he walked her through. "I'm thinking this will be the nursery," he said, showing her the larger of the two upstairs bedrooms. "Of course, the paint color needs to be changed. I'll do that after I close."

Tori stepped in, immediately envisioning pastel and neutral colors in place of the current dark green. She could picture a chair with ballerinas on it for a girl. Perhaps a truck motif for a boy. Maybe Winnie the Pooh bears. The cute teddy was good for either sex. Or maybe no border at all. "It'll be a nice room," she said.

"Glad you approve," Jeff said. "I want you to be comfortable. I mean, the baby will be spending a lot of time with me."

"I suppose so," she said, though the thought still didn't sit well. She'd researched Missouri joint custody laws, and with Jeff in St. Louis and traveling, he probably wouldn't have used all the visitation the state would give him. She might have been able to have the equal split reduced, but with Jeff in Kansas City, the state would have the child alternating residences every so many days.

Jeff sighed. "I just don't know how to make this any easier."

"I know," she said. She reached out and placed a hand on his arm. "I know you are. Most of this is me. I'd planned on moving on with my life when I left St. Louis. Life post-Jeff I guess you could say. Then I found out I was pregnant. Now we'll always share something."

"We shared a lot that was special. I'm not ready to let you go," he admitted.

"Perhaps not," Tori said. "But you can't give me what I want. And I deserve to be happy."

"You do," Jeff said. He shifted his weight as if uncomfortable with the conversation. "I never meant for you to be unhappy. In a sense I'm sorry that my being in Kansas City is making things rough. Then again, I'm not sorry that I'm going to be a father—I'm going to do what's right for my child."

"You're definitely starting to prove it," Tori said. "I hope we can always be friends, it will make life easier for our son or daughter."

He stood there for a moment as if he wanted to say something. Then he swallowed and glanced at his feet. "Let's get out of here and get some dinner. We can talk about these other issues then. Back to the matter at hand. You've seen the room. I want your feedback on how you'd decorate it."

"It's not my house," Tori protested.

"No, but you're the mother. I want your input. What would you do if this was your house and your nursery?"

The words sounded like a trap, but Tori took the bait and began describing the room as she'd decorate it. She grew animated as she talked, and she was aware of Jeff watching her every movement. When she finally finished, they went back downstairs and met up with the real-estate agent, who'd been in the kitchen making calls on her cell phone, and left the house.

Jeff took her to dinner, but didn't bring up the topics raised in the bedroom, and, despite her reservations, Tori found herself enjoying his company. When Jeff wanted to be charming, he could be the best companion in the world. At dinner he made her laugh by cracking jokes and filling her in on gossip about some of their competitors. The food was great, the conversation good and, afterward, Jeff dropped Tori off at Wright Solutions. The lot was bare except for a few cars. Jeff came around and opened her door.

"Thanks for going," he said.

"Thanks for dinner," she said as she climbed out. "I'm stuffed. I don't think I've eaten that much in a long time."

"Then we'll have to do it again," he said, holding the door between them. Tori slid into her car and Jeff shut her door for her. She put the keys in the ignition and rolled down the window. "Drive safe," Jeff said, leaning down. He pressed her door-lock button.

"I will," Tori said.

"Good night then." Jeff straightened, patted the side of her car and moved away.

As Tori drove off into the night she contemplated the turn of events. She'd been close enough to smell his aftershave, yet Jeff hadn't made a move on her. Maybe he was serious about just being friends. The thought both warmed and cooled her ego. Being friends was what she wanted, but Jeff no longer fighting for her was a little deflating. She'd expected some resistance. But maybe his motives were as plain as he said—he just wanted to be a father to his child. After all, he didn't love her, why should he get worked up over her saying she didn't want to marry him? Maybe he was relieved.

And maybe she shouldn't be analyzing this situation so closely; it was starting to drive her crazy. With Jeff, she'd learned that there were no easy answers. And yet he'd changed. Sort of. "Ugh," Tori said, turning up the radio to drown out her tumultuous thoughts. Whatever was going to happen was going to happen. She was pregnant. One thing was clear: there was no turning back now.

"SO LET ME MAKE SURE I heard all this correctly," Joann said, after Tori had told her about the property a week later over the phone. "You went to see his house, loved it, went to a nice dinner and then he dropped you off and left. No kiss. No nothing."

"Nothing," Tori said. "Jeff always tries something but this time he didn't. It was as though we were just good friends. We had the best time, got along great and then, poof, he was distancing himself and heading to his car. I mean, minivan. I told you he bought a minivan, right?"

Even though she'd ridden in it, part of her still didn't believe he'd bought a minivan. The man loved sports cars.

"Yes, you told me about five minutes ago that he got an upscale grocery-getter," Joann said. "Your baby's already eating your brain cells. Just wait until nine months—you won't remember anything. This time *you'll* be the flake."

"Lovely. So what does all this stuff with Jeff mean?"

"It means he's thinking ahead. That's a good trait in a man."

Tori tapped her fingers on the arm of her sofa. She guessed she needed to be more proactive and start finding somewhere to live. "I just don't understand why he's doing this? He doesn't love me. I'm not going to wear down."

"Of course you aren't," Joann said. "You've been in love with him for two years, and now all of the sudden he's turning into Mr. Wonderful. You're wise to question his motives, especially if his feelings haven't changed. The last thing you want is to discover that the prince will turn back into a frog the minute you kiss him."

"I'm not kissing him, so stop poking fun at me," Tori

said. She shifted, her pregnant body beginning to get uncomfortable. The doctor said she'd feel like this.

"I'm not laughing at you, really I'm not," Joann said. "I'm down here eating ice cream and having a pity party for myself. What was I thinking, having four kids? You should see what the boys did to the house and I'm simply too tired to clean anything up. Luckily, Kyle's mom swept in and took the boys away. I needed a rest and some adult conversation."

"Where's Kyle?"

Joann sighed. "He's out picking up some groceries and getting take-out Chinese on the way home. He's a saint. I've been craving sweet-and-sour chicken and steamed rice for weeks. It's all I eat, and unless he fixes something else, that's all he gets. I swear, I have to be having a girl this time."

"I haven't decided whether I want to find out," Tori confided. The friends had become closer during this period, their pregnancies gave them so much more in common.

"I didn't know with my first—made for a fun surprise. No matter what, you immediately fall in love."

"I'm looking forward to that," Tori said. She'd learned that it was normal to dream about the birth and the moment you first held the life you'd created. So far, that had happened several times.

"Prenatal visits going okay?" Joann asked.

"More or less. I've been tired, which I understand is normal."

"I had to have tons of naps with my first," Joann said. "It's normal. Now as long as Jeff doesn't stress you out at the office, you should be fine."

"He's been pretty decent about everything. He's

going with me to my next ultrasound. He's really excited about it."

"He should be. Kyle actually cried the very first time. Now it's old hat."

"I don't know how Jeff will react. He's been so different lately."

"You don't believe it will last," Joann observed.

"I'm a realist," Tori said. "He's only like this because he's trying to convince me to marry him." She stared into the dark woods behind her apartment. "Although he hasn't asked me again."

"Of course that's still his agenda," Joann said. "A man doesn't simply move across the state and buy a new car just because he woke up one day and got an e-mail. He's been crazy about you these past two years and didn't realize it until you were gone. Maybe he's had an epiphany. Goodness knows it took him long enough."

"I doubt that's it," Tori said skeptically. "He's just trying to be charming so that he can get what he wants. Everyone knows you can't change a man."

"Tori, do you love that man?" Joann asked.

"Yes, but…" Tori stopped. She had always loved him. Probably from day one. No matter how much she tried to move on with her life, she'd likely never stop loving him.

"But what?" Joann prodded.

"But…" Tori's voice trailed off again. What she and Jeff had was easy companionship. Baby or no baby, it would never be the kind of love everyone else had. Something would always be missing.

"Stop judging your relationship on everyone else's," Joann inserted, as if reading Tori's mind. "You know he cares for you. Could he grow to love you?"

"I've always maintained that I don't want to win him just because of my own tenacity," Tori said.

"Why not?" Joann asked. "You've been in love with Jeff for what amounts to forever. Now he's yours for the grabbing. He's a good guy. He'll make a good father."

"Well…" That much was true. But it wasn't enough. Tori sighed. "But that doesn't mean I won't come in second, right after his work and his computer. He just came to the office and, you know what? The office hasn't stopped buzzing."

"Honey, he moved across the state to be near you. That's going to cause some excitement and gossip. I'm sure everyone is simply impressed with his dedication and desire to be near you."

"Near the baby," Tori corrected. "When it comes down to it, he's here for the baby, not me."

"He bought a house that you immediately loved. He's planning. He's nesting. He's seeing long-term. Maybe you should give him a chance."

"I don't want to end up being divorced," Tori said. "If I say 'Yes' and it all falls apart, I'll lose and our child will lose out. That's probably my greatest fear."

"Let me play devil's advocate by saying, what about that 'better to have loved and lost than never to have loved at all' saying?" Joann asked. "Date the man for a while. You never really did that."

"Blech," Tori said, giving her opinion on that. "Let me respond by saying it's better never to have tasted cake than to crave it forever."

"You already crave him," Joann said. "You've been miserable. Your choice, Tori."

"You sound like you're on his side."

"I'm on both of your sides," Joann said. "I think you

two need to give nature a little push. What do you have to lose? Date the man, maybe eventually moving into his house and into his bed. He'll fall in love with you. You'll discover you have everything you want."

"That's the worst advice I've ever heard," Tori said. "And even if things went that way, I can't marry him without love first."

"Sweetheart, it's the chicken and the egg. Who cares what comes first so long as you get the omelet? Do yourself a favor. Let him woo you. And when the time is right, don't question things and jump in."

"I can't. He's—"

"He's good father material," Joann cut in. "He'll care for you the rest of your days. You two have fantastic chemistry, which is more than a lot of people have going for them."

"We have nothing in common." Tori's fears claimed her. She'd been trying to get rid of Jeff. She'd wanted to move on and find someone who could love her without reservation. Now he'd moved to be near her just because she was pregnant.

Until she was one-hundred percent positive Jeff was completely in love with her, marriage was the furthest thing from her mind.

"Tori, you have more in common with Jeff than you know. Focus on the positives. Find that girl who went bungee jumping. That girl was fearless. She's still in there, Tori. Just believe."

"That's the trouble," Tori said. "I'm having a lot of difficulty with being that girl lately. Does pregnancy really make you that different? Is that why I feel so paralyzed, fearful and that I'll make the wrong decision?"

"Could be," Joann said.

Tori's doorbell buzzed. "Someone's here." She toted the cell phone with her and peered out the peephole. "It's Jeff."

"So let him in," Joann said.

Tori opened the door. He held up a white paper bag. "Ice cream from Ted Drewes. Chocolate chip. Your favorite."

Tori's mouth watered. Ted Drewes was a St. Louis institution with the best ice cream in town. "How'd you get that?" Tori asked.

"My secret," Jeff said as he entered her apartment. "I'll only tell you it's fresh and is packed in lots of dry ice to keep it frozen."

"Jeff bought me Ted Drewes," she told Joann. "Joann's on the phone," she said to Jeff.

"I love Ted Drewes," Joann said. "What a sweet-heart. You consider what that means—he's thinking of you. Have a good night and I'll talk to you soon. Ciao."

"Joann," Tori began, but her friend had already disconnected. She set the phone down. "So, Ted Drewes?" Tori asked, eyeing the bag.

"Yep," Jeff said. "And the real stuff that you get at their Chippewa location, not what you can buy at the grocery store." His grin did something to her insides.

Her stomach grumbled. Chocolate-chip-custard ice cream, brought all the way across the state. "So you were in St. Louis today," she accused.

He handed her the bag. "Guilty. In all honesty, Justin told me Lauren craved Ted Drewes practically every night during her pregnancy. So I got you the best."

Tori moved into the kitchen and removed the dry ice. Packed in the bag was a yellow quart-sized container with a plastic lid.

"Thank you," she said, humbled by his actions. "This is a real treat. And you're right. I was craving something like this, especially since it's not available here."

"You're welcome," Jeff said. "I aim to help you meet your every craving."

She tamped down the sudden desire she felt and focused on the chocolate-chip ice cream on the counter. Sex had muddled her brain too many times. Tonight Jeff had made a grand gesture and she refused to cloud what he'd done by getting physical. She wanted to be valued for being something other than a bed partner. She wanted the romance. Maybe then they might have a chance.

"Want some?" she asked, dipping her spoon in the container and offering him a bite. The ice cream had traveled well.

"Not necessary," Jeff said. "I actually have to get going."

"Already?" She was stunned. That was it? He brought her ice cream and now he was disappearing? It was so unlike him.

Jeff smiled at her and headed toward the door. "Yep, I'm out of here. I'll see you in the office tomorrow— I've cleared my afternoon appointments so we can go to your ultrasound."

With that, he was gone, leaving her alone to enjoy her treat. She settled down on the sofa, the television providing background noise.

He'd stopped by just to bring her ice cream. She scooped some into her mouth, the frozen custard melting on her tongue. Heavenly. She thought about calling Joann back, but knew what her friend would say.

Tori pondered his actions alone. Once again, he hadn't

kissed her. He hadn't asked her to marry him. He'd simply brought her a gift. He'd never done that before.

As much as she'd like to predict the future, the only certainty was that Jeff wasn't going anywhere and that, in a few months, she'd have a baby. Maybe he *was* changing. Or was it just an illusion? Time would tell, Tori knew. But as she snuggled into bed hours later, she decided that tonight was a good start.

Chapter Nine

"Hi, Jeff, I'm Dr. Hillyer." The doctor shook Jeff's hand as he followed her into her office after Tori's appointment. "It's nice to meet you. Tori mentioned you'd like to be present during the ultrasound?"

"Yes," Jeff said. He was meeting Tori's OB-GYN for the first time and so far he was impressed. Not that Jeff knew much about delivering babies, but Lauren's aunt had sung the doctor's praises to Lauren, and Jeff trusted that his sister-in-law knew what she was talking about. He also trusted Tori, and wished she'd return the sentiment. At least she was letting him attend her doctor's visits. He and Tori were headed to the ultrasound next. It would be the last one unless complications arose. While the doctor's office had most of the necessary equipment, this ultrasound required higher resolution machinery and so Tori was going to a women's health center that specialized in these type of things.

Dr. Hillyer cleared her throat and began speaking. "Well, I just examined Tori and she gave me permission to talk with you. She's doing well. Aside from some minor anemia there are no complications. We'll get an even better understanding of what's going on after today's ultrasound."

Having gotten dressed, Tori entered the doctor's office. She was wearing a cute maternity jumper as she'd started to show, just a tiny mound, but definitely proof that something was growing inside of her. His baby. The thought warmed him. He was going to be a father. While he'd never planned on it happening quite this way, now that it was happening he was determined to be the best father he could be. Tori deserved no less.

He sighed and listened to what the doctor was saying. She was sending Tori for more routine blood work. Nothing to worry about, but Jeff worried anyway. It surprised him how much he cared for her. He'd tried to keep his distance, not wanting to push since he and Tori were making some progress. His mother had always been one of those parents who insisted you eat to stay healthy, and Jeff had found himself wanting to say the same thing to Tori. He wanted to check on her at least once a day, but refrained, especially at the office where he tried to keep things as professional as possible. He still traveled, which meant he didn't see Tori as much as he'd like, but he was making sure he was there for the important stuff, like today's ultrasound.

And when that began, it took his breath away.

"See. No twins," Tori said. She lay back on the table, her stomach exposed and the rest of her covered. The technician dimmed the lights and came over to Tori. Jeff, who stood on the other side of the table opposite the technician, had a clear view of the monitor.

He could see the baby. "Here comes some cold again," the technician said as she used a clear ketchup-like dispenser to squirt more gel on Tori's stomach. Jeff saw Tori's skin twitch under the chill and then the technician pressed a white, microphonelike apparatus on Tori and the picture began to take shape again.

Jeff was fascinated. The screen was black and the baby was outlined in white and shades of gray. The technician measured the top of the head. "This will help your doctor assess your due date and make sure it's still accurate," she said. "This here is a hand. See, it's waving at you." The tech used a pointer to draw a circle around it and then typed the word *hand* over top. "Now let's see what else we can see." Within seconds she'd measured the length of the baby.

Jeff glanced at Tori. She was watching the screen, her gaze focused. As he was standing above her, he had an excellent view of her profile, her head resting on the pillow provided. To him, she'd never appeared more beautiful. Impulsively, he reached down, found her hand and drew it into his. A gentle heat formed and, to his delight, she didn't pull away.

"Look at this great view of the face," the technician said suddenly. On the monitor the baby was face up. Clearly visible were closed eyes, nose and lips. The tech froze the picture, but the image quickly vanished as she continued to move the wand.

"Wow," Jeff said. He'd just seen his child's face, even though his son or daughter wouldn't be making an appearance for some weeks now. It was only the end of August. Tori's December due date was a long way away.

But in that second, Jeff felt a bond he'd never experienced before. He'd created life. Oh, he hadn't known it at the time, but sometimes the best discoveries are surprises.

In that brief moment, Jeff had fallen in love with his…son. "It's a boy," the technician said, placing a circle strategically over the part that proved the child's sex. "You did tell me when we started that you wanted to know."

"We did," Tori said.

A boy. Jeff was having a son. He stared at the image on the screen, the baby so healthy yet fragile inside the womb. Jeff squeezed Tori's hand, realizing as he did that the baby was probably only a little bit longer than her hand when outstretched.

A mixture of protectiveness and responsibility overtook him. The powerful emotions came together and at that moment Jeff knew he loved his son.

The technician had finished the ultrasound; she put the wand away and printed out the pictures. Tori glanced at him then, her eyes glistening with a combination of happy and sad tears. He didn't have to ask her what was wrong. He knew. She loved her son. She loved him. And while Jeff knew that he loved her, as well, he also knew that the love he had for her wasn't the kind she wanted.

Did he love her that way? Could he? He wanted a future with her. He wanted to be a family. Was love really this simple? Never having been in love, he didn't know.

"These are for you," the technician said, interrupting his thoughts and handing him a stack of pictures. Then, directing her attention toward Tori, she said, "Once you get dressed, you're free to go. I'll send your file over to your doctor's office. Have a good day."

Jeff followed the technician out of the room. In the waiting room, he thumbed through the ultrasound pictures—copies of every frozen moment, including a picture of his son's face.

Tori came out a few minutes later, any indication of her earlier tears having vanished. Jeff glanced at his watch. "Are you hungry?" he asked.

"Starved."

His own stomach rumbled; he'd missed lunch. "Then let's go get something to eat. My treat."

"We can go dutch," Tori said.

"Nope," Jeff insisted as he led her to the minivan. "I'm taking you out to celebrate. And to thank you. That was one of the most incredible experiences of my life. I'm honored to be sharing it with you."

"Really, I—"

He cut her off. She was sitting in the front passenger seat and he stood in the doorway, his hand on the steel frame. "It was something incredible."

Her eyes widened. She was so close and, overcome by the emotions he'd just experienced, Jeff longed to do nothing but kiss her. Her lips parted in involuntary invitation, but he resisted and took a step back. "Let's go eat," he said.

If Tori felt any disappointment she quickly masked it. At dinner, she brightened considerably. Not wanting to dull the light mood, Jeff stayed on happy, easy topics and soon the night came to an end and he dropped her off at her apartment.

When he walked her to her door, he didn't kiss her goodbye.

The drive back to his house took about twenty minutes and he'd blared the radio the whole way.

He'd moved into his house early, and now he parked in the garage and used the key to get into the utility room. His cat meowed in greeting and Jeff filled the cat's bowl with dry food. He then wandered through the empty house. His apartment furniture had managed to fill all but two of the rooms. He strode through every area, assessing.

The house needed personalization. If he was going to prove to Tori he was serious about them, and somehow make her believe that he planned to stay and support her, he was going to have to show her he was serious. And it was about time he started.

"SO WHAT ARE WE doing today?" Tori asked. Two weeks had passed since the ultrasound, and in that time Jeff had made a concerted effort to be a regular presence in her life. Tori knew she should probably be resisting, but this "new Jeff" was someone she liked being around. She wanted to spend time with him, especially if he could be a positive influence for their child.

Thus, when he'd asked her earlier in the week, she'd agreed to spend Saturday afternoon with him. Jeff had picked her up, but he still hadn't told her what they were going to be doing. He'd just asked her to bring a set of grubby, could-get-messy clothes.

Those were in the bag on the floorboard. She stretched out her feet as Jeff pulled into the hardware-store lot. "Lowe's?" she asked.

"Our date starts here," Jeff said, grinning. He came around to help her out of the car. "I'd like your help."

"Doing what?"

"Buying paint."

"Paint?" Tori walked beside him as they entered the store. "Why do you need paint?"

"Because my house needs some new color, especially the baby's nursery. That's a top priority. I want you to help me pick out the colors."

"You had me bring clothes," Tori said, putting two and two together. She rolled her eyes. "You knew I'd volunteer to help."

Jeff nodded, his expression guilty. "And you're probably better at it than I am."

"True. But how did you know I could do this?"

"I admit to asking your doctor while you were getting dressed if this type of activity was off-limits. It's not, and I know you like doing home decorating. Since you're the only lady in my life aside from my mother—and her taste tends more toward lace doilies—I figured I'd bribe your assistance with an offer of a gourmet dinner. You had such great ideas for the nursery the day you first saw the house."

"Ah, so now you think I can be bribed." She raised an eyebrow but Jeff didn't look placated.

"Yep, at least I hope so," Jeff said, leading her over to the paint chips. "I was thinking yellow. I mean, just because we're having a boy doesn't mean the walls need to be baby-blue, right?"

"Right, but will he want a yellow room when he grows up? That doesn't seem very manly."

"We can repaint it," Jeff said.

"True," Tori said. "But I was thinking about it and I like the idea of doing the walls more of a tan color. Khaki perhaps. Then accents can be brought in. Red lamps. Trains. Blue sailboats."

"What about a border?" Jeff asked, holding up a brochure.

"If we want more color we can install a chair rail and paint the lower half of the walls another color. That always works. We could even do a stripe." She pointed to one of the displays.

"That's a good idea," Jeff said.

She stopped, paint-company brochure in hand. "Why are you doing all this?"

"Because I want it to be perfect," Jeff said. "I want

the nursery to be the best it can be. I guess I'm doing this for you. For us."

"Why?" she asked him.

"Because you and the baby are important to me and I want to do the right thing. I want to make you happy."

She stood there for a moment, looking at him. There was no mistaking how earnest he was, and this was the first time he'd ever voiced that he wanted to make her happy. "The chair rail will take a bit of work to put up, but we can get the walls painted and the curtains done today," Tori said, as a salesperson came over and helped them find the right paint. Jeff also bought everything else the clerk thought they'd need: spackle, a stepladder, blue painter's tape, drop cloths, paintbrushes, paint pans, rollers and poles.

After checking out, they returned to the house and began to attack the nursery. The house had hardwood floors upstairs, and they placed the drop cloths on it to catch any loose paint.

Tori taped up a windowsill while Jeff worked on edging the ceilings. "The Realtor said they painted the ceilings before I moved in, so we won't have to do that," Jeff said.

"They do look fine," Tori said. He also looked pretty good, cutting an impressive figure standing on the stepladder. She finished the prep work and grabbed a roller. Soon she had half a wall painted. Jeff finished edging and came down to view her work.

"Great job," he said.

"Thanks," Tori said.

She continued to work on the wall. Earlier, she'd changed into her grubby clothes and they already had a few paint splats on them.

Jeff put his paintbrush down and grabbed a roller.

Soon they had all the walls done. They took a moment to survey their handiwork; Jeff reached over and scratched the tip of her nose.

"Hey," Tori said, pulling backward a little, her body reacting to his touch.

"You had paint on your nose," he told her, flipping over his finger to show her what he'd removed. "Couldn't have that."

"I guess not," Tori said.

Jeff reached out and tapped her nose. He moved closer to her, smelling of latex paint and aftershave. "All better now. How about we let this paint dry, change clothes and go out to that dinner I promised you?"

"That sounds like a plan," she said. The butterflies in her stomach were not only from being hungry.

DINNER WAS DELICIOUS, as was the dessert.

"Is it good?" Jeff asked Tori of the chocolate cake she'd ordered for dessert.

"Yes," she said. "One thing about being pregnant is I can eat just about anything I want and I don't have to worry about the calories. I have to admit, I'm loving it."

"You haven't gained that much weight."

"No, but I'm sure I will. My mom lost it all, though, so I'm expecting it'll fall off me. I mean, you lose about fifteen pounds just giving birth."

"Have you given a thought to hospitals and such?" Jeff asked. "I'm willing to help you find one, if you'd like. I've already started asking around for pediatrician recommendations."

"I have all that to do. It's next on my list."

"Let me help," Jeff said. He reached out and covered her free hand. "I'd like to help. Seriously."

"I appreciate that," Tori said. "When I first got pregnant I wasn't sure how much you wanted to be involved. You never seemed too keen on having kids."

"I don't think I was, at least not two years ago when we first got involved," Jeff said. "I'll admit I was pretty selfish—I wanted you all to myself. I didn't really want to think about the future."

"You made things very hard," Tori said.

"I'm starting to realize that now," Jeff said.

Tori slid her hand out from under his. "Just know that there's no pressure coming from this end. I'm grateful for what you're doing, but I'm not expecting anything more."

"I think I'd like to try for something more," Jeff said. "I don't want to lose you, Tori. I was wrong to demand that you marry me, but I want you in my life. You and the baby. I want you both."

"But you don't love me," she said. "Not like Justin or Lauren or even your parents."

"Let's not start that again," Jeff said. "I'm not there, no. It sounds lame. This is new ground for me. I'd like to take things slow. Take the next step. I'm trying to make a home, not just for our son but for all of us. I'll come clean. I'm hoping that eventually you'll move in with me so we can be a family, even if we aren't married."

"Oh," she said, stunned that he was moving so quickly. "So that's the new plan."

"It is," he said. "I'm serious. I want it all, too, and I want it with you."

Which meant, should she choose to accept, that Jeff was asking for the next level. Only he was asking her not because he loved her, but because he *wanted* her without reservation. Could she deal with that?

Could she settle?

"I'll have to think about it," she said.

"Do that," Jeff said. "I hadn't planned on asking you tonight anyway. I didn't mean for it to come out like this. We've skipped a lot of the small stuff, I think."

"We have. I still don't know lots of basic stuff about you," she said, scraping the fork along the bottom of the plate so she could get every last morsel. "I mean, I know the big picture, but not the little things. We've never even dealt with that, which I guess is odd since we were together two years."

"What do you want to know?" Jeff said, his forehead creasing.

"Your middle name," she said. "Things like that." Those details had seemed so unimportant when they'd kept their relationship physical.

"William," he said. "Named for my grandfather."

"Favorite food, besides pizza." Jeff and Tori's Saturday nights had been movie-and-pizza dates. Of course there were a few times that he'd cooked for her, but that had tapered off after the first few months.

"Steak," Jeff said. "I love that stuff, especially homemade. Ribs. Pork steaks. Anything that you grill outside over an open flame, charcoal preferred. Add baked potatoes and corn on the cob and I'm set."

"I see," Tori said.

"Take some time to get to know me again," Jeff said. "I think we'd both like that. We have time before the baby comes."

"I'll think about it," she said.

"Good." He leaned back, satisfied.

But was it good? Tori questioned later, after he'd

dropped her off at home. Could she continue her relationship with him, knowing that she'd never have everything she wanted? That she'd always be missing one essential ingredient, true love?

Chapter Ten

"So when are you going to marry my son?"

Tori blinked and tried to remain calm as she stared at the woman in front of her. They were in Tori's office—at least being on her home turf gave her some comfort.

"Well?" Rose Wright asked.

"Uh," Tori stammered. Jeff's mother had caught her unawares, but Tori could handle this. She and Jeff had forged a better understanding over the past few months. After his surprise of the ice cream and the house painting, they'd taken things slow, almost as if they were starting over and dating. Although Tori's happy hormones had kicked in full force and she didn't know how much longer she could resist, Jeff had not tried to kiss her.

But hormones weren't the only reason she was close to caving. Despite her intention to be just friends, she'd fallen even harder for Jeff. If this new-and-improved Jeff was the real deal, then it was possible they did have a future together. He'd made his house a home, soliciting her decorating advice. He had scaled back travel as promised; he was still gone at least once a week, but that was better than being gone five days a week for weeks at a time.

And, damn him, he was *conveniently* absent today, when his mother had come to town. He had told her that he avoided family visits, hadn't he?

"Jeff and I have an understanding," Tori began, trying to find appropriate words to explain the situation to Jeff's mother, especially when Tori wasn't quite sure herself how to define their relationship, even though it was October. She'd never given Jeff an answer about moving in with him, and he hadn't pressured her to marry him, either.

Rose Wright made a sound in her throat that was a cross between a harrumph and someone choking. "Understanding under-schmanding," she said. "My grandchild needs to have two parents."

Now Tori understood why Jeff hadn't brought her home to meet Mom. For two years Tori had thought it was because she wasn't good enough or because he wasn't serious. Seeing the barely five-foot human tornado in front of her had revealed the truth. Jeff's omission had nothing to do with keeping her in her place. He'd been protecting her. "Your grandchild does have two parents," Tori said firmly. "Jeff and me."

"*Married* parents," Rose amended. She leaned forward and waved her hand in the air for emphasis, making Tori's pounding headache worse. She'd worked through lunch and it was close to three o'clock. Her stomach growled and she wished she had some of the Halloween candy that was all over the stores.

"Didn't you eat today?" Rose asked, those green eyes that were so similar to her twins' narrowing.

"I snacked," Tori said. When Rose frowned, Tori knew she wasn't making a very good first impression on Jeff's mother. Then again, she hadn't been expecting Rose Wright to just show up. She'd claimed she was popping by to see Jeff, but Tori wasn't that naïve, especially when Jeff wasn't even around.

No, Rose had come to scope out the mother-to-be. So far, she clearly found Tori lacking, already she was digging in her handbag and passing a packet of saltines across the desk. "Eat these. I keep them in my purse when I travel. Plane, train or car, it doesn't matter. I get motion sickness."

"Did Jeff know you were coming?" Tori asked.

Rose shrugged. "I'm sure my husband took care of the arrangements. He's at the hotel. We came to do some early Christmas shopping on the Plaza and to see Jeff's new house. I heard he painted the nursery."

"He did."

"Jeff's handy like that," Rose said.

"I wouldn't have believed it until I saw it myself," Tori admitted.

"So when are you moving in?" Rose asked pointedly.

"Uh…" Tori drew a blank. She had her home; he had his. Neither had spent the night with each other since the last time they'd had sex. Eons ago.

"You know he only bought the house because of you," Rose said. She pointed at the package she'd handed Tori. "You need to settle your stomach. It's not good for you to starve the baby. I had three boys. I know."

Tori opened the wrapper and the plastic crinkled. She took a bite, chewed and swallowed. The cracker was fresh, but eating it made her thirsty. "Can I get you something to drink? Bottled water?"

"Thank you. That would be nice," Rose said. She brushed a gray hair off her face. Tori retrieved two bottles and handed one to Jeff's mom. As Rose opened it, Tori took a moment to e-mail Jeff. She typed a simple SOS and hit Send, hoping he was nearby. Then she cracked open the cap on the bottle, ate the other cracker and took a long drink of water, all while enduring Mrs. Wright's scrutiny.

"I figured it was about time we met," Rose said. She leaned forward to shake Tori's hand, something she hadn't done when she'd arrived.

"It probably is time," Tori said with a sigh. "I'm Tori."

Rose nodded. "How have you been feeling?"

"The doctor says I'm perfectly healthy," Tori said. Jeff's mom was rail-thin and impeccably dressed. Tori felt as big as a house in her maternity jumper.

"That's good," Rose said. "Has Jeff been supportive?"

"He's been great," Tori admitted. He had been.

"So is there a future for you two or not?" Rose asked. Tori simply sat there and Rose smiled slightly. "Sorry. I'm very blunt—it's my worst habit—but I've learned it's better to be forthright."

"Well, I'll be honest with you then. I don't know if there is a future for us. Jeff and I haven't talked about it," Tori replied. "I'm not due until the end of the year. I still have to get through November and December and, frankly, Jeff and I have a lot of issues. Private things."

"I understand," Rose said, waving the plastic water bottle around. "I'd prefer you marry him, but…" She let her sentence end there.

"I'd very much like to get married someday," Tori said, getting the impression that Mrs. Wright thought her a heathen. "But as I said, Jeff and I have private things to work through before we consider such a step."

Rose frowned. "He did ask you, didn't he?"

"Yes."

"Then what's stopping you?" Rose said, her eyes sharp.

"Jeff and I aren't ready for marriage," Tori said. "Mrs. Wright, I do love and care for your son, but that doesn't mean that, for us, marriage is the right thing."

"Perhaps not," Rose admitted. "He can be very single-minded. He's a good boy, though, much calmer than his twin. He was never one for spending much time with the ladies, not like Justin. The girls, they were always all over Justin. They phoned constantly during high school—drove us all crazy. Jeff's more focused. Dated one person at a time. Didn't play the field. He knows exactly what he wants when he sees it. However, he has enough bachelor issues that it would take a saint to put up with him. Sometimes I wondered how you did it for as long as you did. I do want you to know one thing, though. If he said you are the one he wants to marry, then you are. Baby or no baby."

"Mrs. Wright..." Tori began, struggling for the perfect words. Then again, what exactly was she trying to communicate? Tori found herself floundering.

"Rose," Jeff's mom corrected. "If you're going to be the mother of my grandchild you should at least call me Rose, as we'll be seeing a lot of each other. I'm planning on being there after the birth if you don't mind. I held each of my grandchildren within hours of their arrival and I'd like to be there for this one. Do you know where you're going to be delivering?" Rose asked.

"I haven't toured the hospitals yet," Tori admitted. With work and seeing Jeff, she simply hadn't gotten around to it. "As I said, I'm not due for a while, so I figured I'd do the hospital search the first week of

November. We've got a new staff member starting in a week and I want to make sure he's acclimated. Once he is, he'll be taking over some of my duties while I'm on maternity leave."

"Babies can arrive early," she said. "My twins did. Make sure you're prepared."

"I will," Tori reassured her. "My mother also gave me a bassinet, wet wipes, diapers and a few sleepers just in case."

"You need to have a baby shower," Rose pointed out. "You need a car seat. Stroller. Blankets. Crib. Changer. And don't forget all those small things like baby monitors and—"

"I believe my mother is organizing something," Tori inserted. At least she thought she was. Her family had been so busy with Kenny's football games that Tori hadn't seen her parents much. That was their life: following all of Kenny's high school sports. If Kenny's team lost, their season would be finished in a week. If not, he could be in the state tournament playoffs around Thanksgiving.

"Let me know when your shower is so I can be there," Rose said.

"Of course," Tori promised. Jeff's mom was actually very nice and Tori's headache had subsided somewhat, which was a relief. She'd been having more and more of them lately, but she'd attributed them mostly to stress. As Rose had pointed out, there were dozens of things to do for the baby's arrival and Tori hadn't gotten to them yet. This weekend she was going car shopping.

She jolted to her feet as her office door burst open and then sighed with relief as Jeff strode into the room. "Mom!" he said. "Great to see you."

Rose stood and he enveloped her in a hug. Her son was a foot taller than her and he seemed to swallow her up. "Did you get your dad's message?" Rose asked.

"Of course," Jeff said. "I've cleared my entire schedule so that I can spend some time with you and Dad now that you're here. I see you met Tori."

As he released her, Jeff caught Tori's eye and winked. She smiled slightly. He'd just confirmed what she'd suspected—he'd had no idea his parents were surprising him with this visit until he'd gotten her SOS message. Tori watched mother and son talk for a moment. She hadn't realized she knew Jeff so well that she could read him as she'd just done.

"Dinner?" he was directing the question to Tori.

She shook her head. "You and your parents go and have fun catching up. I'm going to be working late. I have to get these reports done and you can't keep sidetracking me or Jared will have my hide."

Instead of arguing, he nodded his assent. "Then how about I stop by later? Bring some carryout?"

"Okay," she found herself agreeing. She watched him go, assisting his mother through the door.

"Yes, I bought a minivan," he was telling Rose. "You took a cab here? I'll drive you back to the hotel. No trouble. You can ride in my new car, check it out."

Their voices faded and Tori slumped into the chair. The baby moved, bouncing on her bladder. Groaning, Tori rose to her feet again and headed to the bathroom.

"So, MY MOM DIDN'T intimidate you too much, did she?" Jeff asked later that evening when he stopped by around eight-thirty.

Tori paused mid-dip, her fork hovering over the

takeout box. In addition to the entrée, he'd brought her a piece of three-layer chocolate cake with chocolate icing—her favorite—from the restaurant where he and his parents had eaten dinner.

"Your mom is a dynamo," she said. "You weren't lying."

"Nope. And I guess she had to be, raising my brothers and me," Jeff said. "You haven't met my grandmother yet on my dad's side. She's ninety-two now and has outlived everyone but her two kids. We came for Christmas a few years ago when she was eighty-nine and all she did was harp on my mother about how her grandchildren weren't married. Anyway, my mom thinks Melvin—that's my dad's brother—is the one my grandmother always favored. So my mom says Melvin's side of the family is slightly certifiable."

"Seriously?" Tori asked. The cake was delicious and she took another bite. "Your mom said that?"

"Yeah, she's a hoot. She probably held back today."

"Not really," Tori said, remembering the conversation.

"Oh, really. She has no problems letting the guns blaze when necessary. When you get to know her, you'll realize why we love her so much. She's a powerhouse take-no-bull kind of a lady, but she's put up with a lot. Both of her parents are gone now—they died when she was in her late twenties. As she was an only child, she competed with dozens of cousins growing up. Everyone lived on the same block on the south side of St. Louis. She met my dad in college, and then lost him during his time in the army. She married him within weeks of his return."

"You really admire her."

"Absolutely. She's been our family's backbone for,

well, all of my life. I'm pretty lucky to have parents like mine. They raised me right and I hope to do half as well with my child."

Silence descended and Tori reached out and covered up Jeff's hand with one of hers. "Thanks for sharing," she told him. "You've never opened up to me about your family before. At least, not like this."

"I guess I haven't," Jeff agreed. "When we were together I didn't want to bring anything from the outside in. No stress. No issues. I wanted our time to be focused only on each other. Does that make sense? I wasn't trying to keep you out of my life. I was trying to keep you and I insulated and everything else out."

"I think I understand," Tori said, for she was beginning to see that Jeff hadn't wanted her in a box; he'd only wanted every minute with her to be about them only.

Unfortunately, life didn't work that way, and they hadn't got to know each other in every sense. They'd connected physically. There were some emotions, sure, but she'd let that love connection fall by the wayside when Jeff hadn't returned her feelings, settling into being a woman she'd declared she'd never become.

They'd ignored being more than just sexually intimate. She had always known a lot about what he wanted for his professional future—his goals, his excitement over writing a new computer program—but she didn't know what he wanted for his personal life.

Jeff reached forward and flicked his forefinger over her upper lip. "You had some cake stuck to it," he said. He held up his fingertip and, sure enough, there was a dark crumb attached to it. "Want it?"

She shook her head and instead of brushing it off, he

put his fingertip in his mouth and sucked the cake off. Tori's brown eyes darkened and her legs clenched. Chocolate cake and happy hormones. "Don't do that," she muttered.

"Why not?" Jeff asked. "This is the closest I've been to your lips in ages."

"Don't say *lips*." Tori's full attention was focused on his and she groaned.

"What's wrong?" he asked.

"Happy hormones," she said. And they were demanding satisfaction.

"You don't *look* happy," Jeff observed.

"That's because I'm not," she said. "I'm frustrated. Joann says some women get all…" Tori winced.

He arched his eyebrow. "All what?"

"Full of desire," she admitted softly. "Because of their hormones."

"Horny," Jeff said. His smile split wide.

"For lack of a better term, yes," Tori said, her feathers ruffled. "That just sounds so crass, but that's exactly what it is. What I am."

"So you're frustrated," he said. "You want me. Are you admitting it?"

"Uh…" This conversation was pure torture.

"You did go cold turkey," he said. "We were having sex pretty regularly and then—"

"Don't say *sex*," Tori protested. "I don't want sex. I mean, I do. The doctor says I can have it. But I don't want to have sex just so that I'm physically satisfied. I want more."

"Of course you do," Jeff said. He reached out and traced her upper lip. "That's why I haven't kissed you even though I want to. That's why I haven't touched you even when I'm craving you." He slid his finger down her neck to right above her breast before withdrawing his hand. "They've already gotten bigger. Probably more sensitive, too."

Tori's body shook from the sensations flowing through her. "You—" She couldn't even continue.

"You want me," he said.

"Yes," she spit out, her frustration complete. All he had to do was glance at her and she'd melt, and this time he'd done so much more. "I want you. And if you don't kiss me now, I'm going to die."

"I wouldn't want that," Jeff said, and he lowered his mouth to hers.

CHOCOLATE. She tasted like chocolate cake and magic. He'd never experienced anything so divine. Maybe absence did make the heart grow fonder because Jeff's was now pounding. Other parts of him throbbed as well, and he understood what Tori had meant about need. He'd needed her for a while. He just hadn't realized how much.

He dipped his tongue into her mouth; he used his lips to pull hers into his. She shuddered. She was beautiful.

He knew she'd never believe he really cared about her, but he'd determined to spend his life trying. He, too, wanted it all. That meant Tori and his baby. The whole package.

With more agony than he'd ever known, he broke off the kiss. Her eyes fluttered open, the brown orbs reflecting her confusion. "That's it?" she said, and he sensed her disappointment.

"Yes," he said. "I want it all, too."

She forced herself more upright, scooting back slightly on the sofa so she could see him. "What?"

"I want you to marry me," he repeated. "Marry me and you can have everything you want."

She shook her head and his heart broke. "You sound like your mother. You don't love me."

Although he was pretty sure he was falling in love with her, he didn't deny her statement. To say he loved her—in all that word meant—would ring false. So he told her the truth. "Tori, I want you more than any other woman I've ever known. You haunt my thoughts. I want nothing more than for us to be some sort of a family. To get to know each other for the rest of our lives."

She stared at him, her eyes wide. "You're serious."

"Never more so," he said, meaning every word. "Look at us. We have chemistry. We have tons in common."

"I don't know if that's enough," she said.

"All I know is that I can't continue this way," Jeff said. "I want you. The proof is right there." He saw her glance at the bulge in his jeans. "But I don't want just a sexual relationship. I want more."

Her lips opened and he longed to kiss her, but held back. "You want more?" she asked.

"Yes, I do," he said, for he knew exactly what he wanted. Her. "We'll grow to love each other the way you want. Everything's there to make that happen."

She didn't say anything, and he reached out and grabbed her hand. "I'm sorry if I can't do better than that."

"I need to think," she said.

"I understand." He stood. He hated leaving her, but he knew that he had to see this through. Too much was at stake if he didn't. Within minutes he was out the door.

"He just walked out?" Joann asked.

"Yes." Within minutes of Jeff's leaving, Tori had

broken into tears and called her friends. Lisa and Cecile hadn't answered, but Joann had. Tori sniffled and wiped her nose. "He was kissing me and then he stopped. He told me he wanted everything and walked out."

"Wow," Joann said. She sounded flabbergasted. "Honey, he may love you, even if he doesn't know that's what it is."

"So why did he leave?" Tori asked. Boy, her hormones were out of whack. She'd never been weepy. "Jeff always walks away. He's always traveling, even if he does bring me ice cream or chocolate cake. The only way we ever connected was sexually. Now I don't even have that."

"Maybe this proves he's changing. Perhaps he's only giving you the space you asked for."

"I feel like a ping-pong ball."

"Sweetie, do you still love him?"

"You asked me that last time," Tori said, blowing her nose.

"Marry the man," Joann said. "Give him what he wants. Give yourself what *you* want."

"You think I'm being stubborn." Tori blew her nose again, the sound pathetic. She really was a mess.

"Yes, I do," she said. "I bet if you call him and say yes he'll jump right back in that car and come over."

"I'll think about it," Tori said.

"Do that. Remember that commitment is scary, but you've been committed to him for over more than two years."

"That got me in trouble before. How can I be sure this time will be any different?"

"You won't. But you need to follow your heart, Tori."

Tori suddenly heard a loud crash in the background and Kyle's voice yelling, "Joann. Help!"

"Something's wrong," Joann said. "I've got to go. You keep me posted, okay?"

"Okay," Tori said. She hung up the phone and let the fresh tears come. About five minutes later she was all cried out but no closer to an answer.

Was Jeff really changing? He was already so different and, to her mind, for the better. Even his walking out was uncharacteristic of the man he used to be. She lifted the container that held the chocolate cake and used her finger to get at the last of the icing. Of course, that reminded her of his touching her and she fought back another round of tears.

Sex had been the only way she'd been connected to him before. Now he was making an effort to go further, and in doing so he'd rewritten the program. Gone were the old rules of interaction. She was in unfamiliar territory, unsure of what was real. He was right about one thing. *She* couldn't go on like this.

Chapter Eleven

"Thanks again, Mr. Myoto." As Wright Solutions' newest client rose to his feet, ending the meeting, Tori rose, as well. She walked her guest to the elevator and saw him on his way.

"Nice job," Jeff said. He'd been in the meeting, too.

"Thanks," Tori said. She frowned slightly. She'd been having the worst indigestion all day, and now that lunch had passed, it wasn't getting any better.

"So are we on for doing some baby registry stuff tonight?" he asked, following her to her office.

"I don't know," Tori said. "I haven't been feeling well today."

"What's wrong?" Jeff said, immediately concerned.

"Sour stomach," she said. "Must have been something I ate."

He grimaced. "Take the rest of the afternoon off. You and I can register for baby gifts later if you want. Go home and get some rest. That's the best idea. You do seem a little pale." They walked into her office and he shut the door behind him. "I'd feel much better if you took it easy today."

"I have too much to do to take time off. I'm behind here and I'm starting to worry that I'm falling behind at home. I should have been more prepared. It's the first week of November and I haven't done much. You've done it all."

She sank into her desk chair. Needing a drink of water, she rose. Suddenly she felt a little faint. An intuitive, instinctive feeling grabbed hold of her.

Something was wrong.

Her eyes widened as a muscle-tightening cramp shot through her abdomen and traveled to her toes. This was no indigestion. Her quick intake of breath must have alerted Jeff.

"Tori, what is it? You're as white as a sheet." Genuine concern radiated in his green eyes. "Are you okay? What do you need?"

She needed… She winced as another clutching pain shot through her.

"Are you okay?" she heard Jeff ask again, but his voice seemed disembodied as if floating nearby.

"I don't know," she said, her voice wavering with false bravado.

Surely these pangs weren't contractions. The baby could not be coming now, she wasn't far enough along. She'd had no complications. No problems. Except for her mild anemia—and she took extra iron for that—she was in perfect condition.

Jeff's eyes were studying her, his concern unmasked. "Tori," he said, stepping forward.

"Jeff!" Tori's anguished cry cut through the room like a bullet. "Jeff, I'm—"

But words were useless as Tori realized that her water had broken.

"We need an ambulance," she heard Jeff direct someone at the door of her office.

Tears streamed down Tori's face. The pain sharpened, nearly doubling her over. Jeff moved to her side and she clutched his arm. "Jeff. No. It can't be now."

He didn't understand; he reached forward and tucked a loose strand of dark hair behind her ear. "Shh, Tori, Darci has called 911 and asked for an ambulance. You'll be fine."

"No. The baby. It's way too soon."

His face paled as the impact of her words dawned. "Too soon?"

She dug her fingers into the fine fabric of his sleeve. "It's still too early."

A million emotions flitted across Jeff's face in an instant. He was a powerful man, but her words had stripped him of all control. "Tori, I—"

"Everything will be fine. The paramedics are on their way," Darci reassured them as she came into the office and reached Tori's side. "Doctors often get these due dates wrong. They were four weeks off with my friend's son. Heck, if she'd delivered him on her due date he would have been more than ten pounds."

Another pain overtook Tori and she cried out. Her fingers clutched Jeff's arm tighter. He tensed. "Darci, call my brothers and let them know that Tori's baby is on the way."

"Call my mom, too," Tori managed.

As Darci left the office, Jeff shifted so that he supported more of Tori's weight. The fact that her lower half was damp was irrelevant to him and he gathered her into his arms. "How are you holding up? You're going to be just fine. You're strong, Tori. The strongest woman I know."

He kept talking to her, pausing only when the paramedics arrived and rolled a stretcher into her office. After asking her a flurry of questions, the paramedics helped her onto the stretcher. Soon they had her hooked to several mobile monitors and had inserted an IV into her hand just below her left wrist. The vital-symptom readings that they called out to each other meant nothing to Tori.

Another pain stabbed through her and she shrieked.

"Contractions intensifying and two minutes apart." The female paramedic smiled and Tori heard a click. The stretcher gave a shudder as it began to move.

"Away we go," the paramedic said. "Now don't you worry. I've delivered quite a few babies, so I could do yours, but we'll get you to the hospital in plenty of time for a doctor to do it. Why don't you just close your eyes and rest?"

"Rest," Tori repeated as she closed her eyes. She lost track of Jeff.

"That's right. Close your eyes. There you go. Breathe into your contractions. They always intensify after a woman's water breaks. No, don't try to open your eyes now. I'm nothing that you need to see. All we're doing right now is lifting you into the ambulance."

In the darkness Tori heard a different voice say, "Blood pressure still elevated but steady."

"See, already you're doing much better," the female paramedic told Tori. "Now think happy thoughts, my dear. In just a short while you're going to have a beautiful baby and…"

Tori tuned her out as a firm hand gripped hers. Heat fused between their flesh, joining their fingers together. Jeff. "I'll meet you there," he said. "I'll be right behind the ambulance."

Her words came out a mere whisper. "Please don't leave me."

"I won't. I'll be there," he said. There was a jolt and the trip to the hospital began.

Tori thought she must have dozed through parts of the journey, for the next thing she knew she was in a room with too many bright lights. Had they given her something in her IV to cut the pain? The pang shooting through her body didn't feel as sharp. And why wasn't she pushing? Wasn't she supposed to be pushing or something?

"Is she going to be all right?" She heard Jeff's voice again. She tried to open her eyes, but found she couldn't focus.

"She and the baby are going to be just fine. But the baby is in breech position. We're also worried that the baby may have RDS."

Tori heard Jeff inhale sharply. "What does that mean?"

"Respiratory distress syndrome. Once out, the baby could have difficulty breathing because his lungs aren't fully developed. RDS can also happen if fluid gets into his lungs. I know it's hard, but try not to worry. Complications aren't that uncommon, but we're not taking any chances. I've been in contact with her doctor and we're prepping Tori for an immediate caesarean section.

"Sorry, we can't have anyone but medical personnel in the operating room during surgery. You'll need to remain in the waiting area just down the hall. I promise someone will get you immediately."

A different voice. "This way, Mr. Wright. If you could follow me."

Tori felt a quick kiss on her forehead. "I'll be right outside, Tori. Right outside. You're going to be just fine. You won't feel anything. You and the baby are going to be just fine, just fine."

He said the words again, almost more to convince himself than to reassure her. For a moment, sound seemed to amplify in Tori's ears and she heard his footsteps walking away.

"I'm ready with the general."

"Go ahead."

Panic clawed at Tori. *Oh, I'm so sorry, Jeff. For everything. I should have told you sooner. I should have taken better care of myself. Don't leave me, Jeff! Don't leave me and the baby.* But as her world faded into black, no words left her silent lips.

EVER SINCE HIS BIRTH, Jeff had been the fringe member of his family. He'd been the computer geek, the numbers guy. His father had told him that he had exhibited his destiny early. As a child, Jeff had wanted to read newspapers rather than books. He'd learned numbers before letters and discussed and solved complex problems as young as the age of three. He'd had trouble making friends with kids who just wanted to talk about mud pies or play with G.I. Joe action figures.

He'd never been a chick-magnet like his brother Justin, who'd driven their mother crazy with his revolving-door relationships. Jeff had enjoyed technology and problem solving more than socializing. He hated to make small-talk for conversations' sake.

When he did date, the women often took off after one or two months, complaining that he worked too much or that they couldn't understand him. He took life one day at a time, as it came. Slow and steady. No rush. All problems had solutions.

An irate Greek girlfriend had once called him a *vrahas,* a rock that sat at the edge of the ocean and was pummeled by wave after wave. But the rock was immovable. It was imperturbable, never daunted by the constant battering of the endless sea, It withstood all the furies unleashed upon it. She hadn't meant it as a compliment, but Jeff had taken it that way. He liked being unfazed. And, for the most part he had been, until Tori.

Jeff paused as his heart clenched. A strand of his red hair dared to fall into his face, and, with his left hand, he pushed it back impatiently.

The events in Tori's office had been eye-opening. The moment her water had broken, fear had rooted itself deep in his soul, and his reaction wasn't caused only by his worry for his baby's survival. He was afraid for Tori. She'd got under his skin. He loved her.

To know that he loved her—really loved her—was something of a revelation. Maybe he'd needed something this cataclysmic all along to open his eyes to his own idiocy. He loved her.

He didn't want to lose her.

Trouble was, he already had. While he'd come to Kansas City to woo her and win her, his motivation had been to make his life easier. He'd cared, but hadn't necessarily understood the stakes. Until now.

And now, when he could make the declaration in all honesty, he knew that Tori wouldn't believe him. While he might have shown her he'd changed and that he'd be a good father, nothing he'd done had really shown her he'd make a loving husband in every sense of the word.

She'd been right when she insisted he kept her in a box he'd delegated for her. He had no reasons why he couldn't fall in love with Tori, except for the lame excuse that he hadn't. He'd been like an ostrich sticking his head in the sand. He'd been a fool, and he'd just about lost the only thing in his life that truly mattered.

He paced the empty waiting room. His long stride took him to the end and back in only five movements, and walking did little to soothe his frayed nerves.

Because Tori had had an emergency C-section and had been put under general anesthesia, Jeff hadn't been allowed into surgery. To keep the waiting-room craziness down, Tori's parents were coming tomorrow and Jeff was to call them the moment he got any news. They were probably calmer than he was. C-sections were routine procedures, but that didn't make him feel any better. The baby was early and Tori's face had been ashen.

Stress like he'd never experienced before consumed him. A cold sweat broke out on Jeff's forehead and he stopped pacing the waiting area as a raw and unbridled panic swept through him. The vending machine against the far wall hummed, creating a neurotic buzz that seemed to grow louder until it filled the stark, empty room. A shadow flickered in the corner, the water fountain chose that moment to gurgle and Jeff swore he could almost hear fate laughing at him.

Determined, Jeff brushed off his temporary irrationality. He trusted medical science. He trusted reasoning, especially his own. He had to trust that the doctors and nurses were the best. He had to trust that the baby would be fine. Tori would be okay. Everything would be normal once again and he could go back to slow and steady, with some exceptions. He was going to start proving to Tori that he was the man for her, this time for the right reasons.

Jeff calmed his breathing and banished his panic. He

glanced at his watch and frowned as the hour hand moved again. How long had they been here? How long did the procedure take?

"Mr. Wright?" A doctor in green scrubs entered the waiting room. "Congratulations. It's a boy. Both the mother and child are doing fine…" The doctor paused and Jeff tried to read the man's guarded expression.

At times like these, Jeff was not a patient man. "Tell it to me straight," he demanded.

The doctor took a long breath before beginning. "Miss Adams is doing fine. The baby, however, has respiratory distress syndrome as we feared it might. That means his lungs haven't fully developed, at least not enough to work normally on their own. It's very common in premature babies. We have your son hooked up to a ventilator. It's just a precaution. Usually within a few days to a week they're able to breathe just fine on their own."

Jeff tried to comprehend it all. "He can't breathe?"

The doctor shook his head. "Not the way a baby brought to term can, no. Without the help of a ventilator, he'll have trouble breathing and his lungs will have to work too hard. But there are positives. We're encouraged by his weight. He's six pounds and that's a good sign. We have a top-notch neonatal ICU and we'll make sure he gets excellent medical care. We have a fine staff, one of the best in the area."

Jeff swore under his breath as guilt plagued him. Although the doctor hadn't said the words, Jeff knew the situation could have been much worse.

The doctor cleared his throat. "I know that you're probably having a difficult time taking this all in, so I'll be happy to answer any questions you might have later

or you can ask your pediatrician. He'll be by in the
morning, as will Tori's doctor. As for Tori, we've moved
her to recovery. We've woken her up to make sure she's
fine, but she needs her sleep. Would you like to see
her?"

"Yes." Jeff nodded and followed the doctor through a
short maze of hallways before they paused outside of a
closed door. Tori had been moved to a private room in the
maternity ward where she could recover for a few days.

"She's in here." The doctor held the door open so that
Jeff could enter. "If you have no other questions…?"

Jeff didn't answer the doctor. Both knew there was
no need. As Jeff stepped into the dim room, he saw her
immediately. Even in the low light, he could tell she was
sleeping. He stepped closer. Her skin was so pale.

Her breathing was slow and steady and Jeff assumed
that was a good sign. He went to stand by her bedside
and just watched her for a long moment. He'd never
seen her look so helpless and fragile.

He reached forward and brushed her short brown
hair away from her face. She didn't stir and, as he stood
there, raw emotion overtook him. He loved her. Hopefully it wasn't too late for them.

"Oh, Tori, I'm sorry," he said.

His knees weakened, and he slumped down into the
sterile armchair beside her. He should have done more.
Done it sooner. Treated her more tenderly. Given her the
love she needed. He hadn't loved her soon enough.

Weariness filled him. All he had for his failure were
words. "I'm sorry, Tori. I'm so sorry."

Chapter Twelve

The first thing Tori sensed when she regained consciousness was that something was missing. Her head hurt, her mouth felt dry and cottony and…

Without even opening her eyes, Tori's fingers flew to her stomach. She pressed and felt nothing. Nothing kicked. Nothing bulged against her skin. There were no sensations at all. The baby was gone.

"Shh," an unfamiliar voice said. Tori felt a cool, damp cloth touch her head. "It's nothing to worry about. You've been twisting in your sleep for a while. That's not good for you. Everything's fine. The baby's just fine."

Tori tried to sit up, but nothing in her body seemed to be working. Why couldn't she move?

"Just relax. Everything's okay," the kind voice soothed again. "I'm Sandra, your nurse. You've had a C-section and your body is still experiencing the after-effects. But don't worry. You're doing great."

Tori struggled to sit up but her stomach muscles refused to cooperate and she found herself still lying flat on her back.

"My baby," she said. Her dry mouth made the words hard to voice. "I need to see…I want to see my son."

She felt Sandra's fingers on her wrist as she took Tori's pulse. "Of course you do. He's a sweet little six-pound baby boy. Now if you don't work yourself up, I can take you to him in a little bit. You've just had major surgery. You've been resting a while, but you're still very weak. Your son needs you to have all your strength."

"I want to go now," Tori said stubbornly one last time before she resigned herself to the nurse's directives. She attempted to focus her eyes but failed. She'd always been terrible with anesthetics. She'd had her wisdom teeth out at nineteen, and although she didn't have any swelling, she'd hung her head out of her boyfriend's car window like a dog the entire way home. Even her arms had felt like leaden weights. Tori closed her eyes. "Tell me about my son," she said.

"He's doing great," Sandra repeated. "Rest a bit more and I'll take you to the NICU so you can see for yourself." She pronounced the word Nick-U.

"What's that?" Tori asked.

"The neonatal intensive care unit. Now come on. Don't panic or try to sit up. You're still fragile. You've only been on our floor about fourteen hours."

Fourteen hours? Had she been asleep that long? She vaguely remembered people waking her up and talking to her, but she couldn't recall what the conversations had been about.

Where was Jeff anyway? She twitched slightly. Instead of her baby being with her as she assumed would have happened after a normal delivery, her baby was in the intensive care unit. Despite the nurse's reassurances, Tori knew that something must be wrong if her child was in the NICU.

And instead of being able to do anything, she was stuck here with her arms and legs feeling as if they'd been glued down. At least she wasn't drooling. Tori finally got her eyes working and the hospital room came into view. The nurse held a cup full of water to Tori's lips. "I want to see my son," Tori repeated.

Sandra smiled. "Of course you do, but your doctor is on her way and so is breakfast. Now drink up and I promise you'll get to see him soon, but you won't be of any use for your son if you've collapsed. Now I've got some crackers for you to eat until your meal arrives, which should be any moment. I chose the menu for you, but you can fill out your own lunch and dinner order. I see that crease in your forehead. Now before you worry yourself into a tizzy, the NICU is right down the hall."

Tori drank the water. "What time is it?" she finally asked.

"Eight o'clock," Sandra said. "You slept the whole night. That's a good sign you're well on your way to a perfect recovery."

"My son," Tori persisted. "He's doing all right?"

"You can judge for yourself right after breakfast," the nurse promised as a hospital staff member brought in Tori's breakfast tray. "And don't you worry. Jeff is with your son. He's been here all night. Ah, here's your doctor to check on you."

"Hi, Tori," Dr. Hillyer said. "I hear you've had an adventure. Let's see how you're doing."

IT WAS ABOUT AN HOUR LATER when Sandra finally wheeled Tori to the NICU. Dr. Hillyer had checked Tori over and told her she was recovering well. Sandra had then insisted she eat. Although Tori had little appetite and nothing looked tempting, she forced herself to drink her orange juice and finish her banana—the last thing Tori wanted was to collapse again. While she'd been eating, her son's pediatrician had stopped by and explained RDS. Tori now understood what had happened and why her baby wasn't with her.

"Your son is actually doing great," Sandra said as she stopped outside of the NICU and had Tori wash her hands. "He's a healthy weight and that's very encouraging. I'm sure he's excited to meet you."

The NICU was unlike anything Tori had expected. It was a large room complete with multiple stations—each with one nurse sitting in the middle of four or five bassinet-warming units. Everywhere Tori looked, machines beeped and mothers in rocking chairs held and cooed at their babies. The room hummed with an overabundance of noise.

Tori instinctively knew that there must be more than one NICU—nowhere could she see any truly tiny at-risk babies.

Sandra handed Tori a name tag and Tori attached it to her gown. "Your name tag shows where your baby is in the room and what medical condition he has. Now you follow me. See? There's Jeff. He was with you in your room all night, coming here when we let him, and only after we convinced him that you were fine. He's very devoted and, if I may say so, wonderful with your son."

Tori blinked, her gaze easily locating where Jeff sat in a wooden rocking chair, a small blanket-wrapped bundle pressed to his chest. His concentration focused on the baby, he hadn't noticed Tori yet. Tori held up her hand, stopping the nurse from wheeling her forward. She'd never seen Jeff like this.

As much as she'd dreamed or pictured the moment he'd hold their son, her thoughts had never come close to the reality. The sight of Jeff holding their son pulled on her tender heartstrings. Perhaps she'd always known, deep down, despite what she'd told him, that he'd be a natural father. What she saw confirmed it. Once again, an example of where she hadn't believed.

"So, little man," Jeff said, "they tell me that you're doing great. You probably worried your mom a lot, but she's tough, one of the toughest women I know. She stared a big bear down once. Ah, but maybe I don't remember the story right. It might have been a dog. She'll be here soon, I'm sure. I know she's anxious to see you."

"I am," Tori said and the nurse wheeled her forward.

Jeff glanced up, something new and unreadable in his green eyes. He quickly masked his expression. "Look, big guy, what did I tell you? Here's your mom now."

Tori reached out her arms and Jeff leaned forward. His hands brushed hers and finally the soft, swaddled baby rested in her arms.

She fingered the blanket so that she could see her child. All she could see was his little red face, the rest of him hidden underneath the small teddy bears decorating the receiving blanket. But seeing her son, even with oxygen tubes taped to his face, was enough.

"He's beautiful," she said. "He's so beautiful." Her vision blurred as she began to cry.

"Shh," Jeff said. He rose out of the rocking chair and leaned on Tori's wheelchair. The nurse discreetly straightened out the baby's tubes and he opened his mouth and made a fishlike pucker. His eyes remained tightly closed the entire time.

"Just watch him. He's feisty and strong and he keeps trying to remove his tubes—that's why we have them taped to his cheeks," Sandra advised before moving away to tend to another family.

Tori's tears fell freely; because her hands were full from holding her son, Jeff took a wad of clean tissues from his pocket and wiped Tori's cheeks.

"He's so little," she said. Nothing in her entire life had prepared her for the unbridled emotions flowing through her. She and Jeff had created a person, and the love emanating from her for this tiny, vulnerable life overwhelmed her. More tears came to her eyes. "I should have taken better care of myself. I should have… Oh, I'm so sorry, sweetie."

Jeff placed his forefinger under Tori's chin and gently tilted her face so she could see him. "Don't cry. The nurses say he's doing even better today than yesterday. He'll be going home with us very soon." Jeff's voice caught in his throat and he coughed to clear it. His eyes darkened. "He's very beautiful."

"He is." *Like his father.* Although… A dark shadow of stubble graced his tired face and he was wearing the same clothes he had on the other day. He needed a shower and a shave. The nurse had been right—he had been here all night.

Seeing him so devoted caused more tears to spill down Tori's cheeks. Her baby's nose barely wrinkled as a wayward teardrop touched his skin. She moved the blanket, seeing the white heart-monitor circles taped to his chest. Except for a diaper, her son was naked; the monitors and tubes made wearing baby clothes impossible.

The nurse showed up again. "Time for a check," she said. "It'll take only a minute and I promise you can have him right back."

Tori's arms felt barren the moment she passed her child over. The nurse drew a blood sample by pricking her son's heel. Tori winced.

Jeff stepped behind her wheelchair and put his hands on her shoulders. "He'll be in your arms before you know it. I've watched them work with him for hours now. Don't worry. He's getting excellent care."

Tori reached up; her right hand, seeking comfort, covered Jeff's. She sighed into him and turned her head so that her cheek rested on their joined hands. Jeff used to be her escape, someone to hang out with on the week-ends, but over the past few months their relationship had changed. He'd become her support system.

A movement far away at the NICU doorway caused Jeff to stiffen. Tori straightened and turned her head. Justin. What was he doing here?

"Justin's here to get the office straightened out for us. One of our clients had a small crisis last night that he and I have to deal with so we can get things ready for your maternity leave," Jeff said. He removed his hand and stepped away, the tender moment between them over. "Stay here as long as you want. The nurse will wheel you back to your room whenever you're ready. I'll come back to see you both as soon as I can. Why don't you think of a name while I'm gone and we can talk about it when I get back?"

Tori averted her face as disappointment raced through her. She knew he was right and that she'd left the office in a lurch, but surely someone else could have handled the client. They'd hired a new person for this contingency. Despite the warmth in the room, a chill enveloped Tori as she watched Jeff stride to the doorway, sign out and leave with Justin.

The nurse finished the neonatal check and brought back Tori's son. She smiled and lowered the baby into Tori's arms. "He's doing so much better. You'll both be going home before you know it."

Tori turned her attention to the tiny person in her arms and forced herself to relax so that her son didn't sense her runaway emotions. Taking care of herself and him was the important thing now. Although Jeff had shown her a different side to himself, Tori couldn't let her guard down yet. He'd just raced off on business, yet Tori knew that didn't matter anymore. Her priorities had changed.

She was now a mother, the one most responsible for the innocent, defenseless child she held in her arms. She'd given him life and he needed her. From here on out that would be her focus.

WHEN JEFF RETURNED to the hospital, Tori's maternity room was empty. He found her in the NICU, the baby snuggled up to her chest. She'd moved into the rocking chair; the wooden runners glided easily as she rocked back and forth.

A lump formed in his throat as strange feelings traveled through him. He was in agony. Not even the work he usually loved had been any kind of solace for the concern he felt today. It had taken him away from Tori, probably once again confirming to her that she wasn't a priority in his life. While that was untrue, Jeff knew things were all about perception. He and Tori had become like one of those Hollywood couples you saw on TV. They cared about each other, but career and misunderstandings simply got in the way and sucked the life out of the relationship. Talking didn't help. Only actions would do. Even though he had a lot of ground to make up, Jeff was—thankfully—getting a second chance and the gift of time. He wasn't going to let her down again.

"You're back," Tori said when she saw him. Exhaustion etched her face. "I expected you to be later. Everything go all right?"

"Yeah, the problem was easier to handle than I thought. One last thing I needed to do before I could take some time off. I'll fill you in later, although Justin wanted me to tell you that everything's under control in your absence and will be waiting for you when you return."

"That's good," Tori said.

"It is." He assessed her. "You seem tired. You aren't overdoing it, are you? Your doctor said you shouldn't overexert yourself."

"I'm fine," Tori said.

"Fine." Jeff managed not to scoff at the word. Tori could be so stubborn. He softened his tone. "You had major surgery. Your abdominal muscles have been sewn back together and need to heal. You are definitely not fine by my definition of the word."

Fire lit her brown eyes. "Tough," she said.

Jeff raked his hand through his hair. "You're someone I care deeply about. A great deal. I'm concerned about your welfare."

She stared at him. Even to his ears, those words sounded lame now that he understood the true extent of his feelings. But a declaration of love here would be received as forced. He had to do it in the right place at the right time.

The baby's face puckered and he began to whimper. Tori scowled. "You're upsetting him."

Jeff attempted to relax. "I didn't mean to upset him."

Tori ran her hands over the baby's back as she conceded that point. "I know. I'm just testy. Maybe it's all my own stress coming out. I wasn't prepared for this. I thought I had more time."

"We all did," Jeff soothed. "I had an emergency or I wouldn't have left. Everyone at the office was scrambling, but they handled it like troopers. You've trained them well."

"Thanks," she said.

"It'll all be fine. I'm trying."

"I know. But maybe it doesn't matter anymore," Tori said. "We have to put our son first. Not us."

"Don't say that," Jeff said. He lowered his voice. "Let's not go backward. We've been forging a future. Look around this room and see all the other couples who care about each other. I know you want what they have and I want that, too. Trust me, we'll get there."

She wasn't going to hold out and wait for him to love her. She needed to move on. She'd always love him, but the baby in her arms deserved all of her attention. Loving Jeff, that dream could die. From here on, she'd try to see him as the father of her son, nothing more.

Tori shook her head. The painkillers were making her fuzzy. "Let's just drop this for now."

Something about her tone struck him and he gazed at her. "You don't seriously mean that."

Tori lifted her chin. "I'm sure talking about our

future will come up again, but don't worry. I've finally accepted that you may never fall in love with me. Besides, my feelings seem rather irrelevant when other things—" she nodded at their son "—are so much more important."

Jeff stared at her.

"I'm tired," Tori said. "I know that, in the end, we both want only what's best for our son. We'll work that out."

His chest constricted. "I'm not going to be a virtual parent, only there part-time. I plan to be there for you and the baby, Tori. He'll be safe and cherished. So will you. Please believe me when I say that."

"I'll try," Tori said. "But we don't have a good track record."

"I know," Jeff conceded. "But these past few months have been different. It's a start."

Chapter Thirteen

A week later, Jeff's minivan wound its way through city traffic to his house. Her house, too, Tori admitted as she watched the scenery go by. While she'd been in the hospital her mother had packed up everything she'd thought Tori might need and moved it over to Jeff's place. Because of the C-section, her doctor had told Tori she couldn't do stairs, eliminating her loft as a place to recuperate unless she wanted to sleep on the couch. So she'd agreed to move into Jeff's temporarily, something she'd been thinking about even before the baby's unexpected arrival had made it the most practical option. Besides, he had worked so hard to change the house into a home, and she had happy memories of painting the nursery.

So she was moving into Jeff's bedroom, the bassinet waiting next to the king-size bed in which she slept alone. Jeff had taken another room upstairs.

They'd decided in the hospital to name their son Brendan, and while Tori had been discharged after the standard seventy-two hours, her son had needed to remain in the NICU a few extra days so he could have phototherapy, a light treatment for the jaundice he'd developed.

She'd hated being separated from him. It had taken all of the NICU nurses and Tori's doctor to persuade her that she needed adequate rest and that she should return with Jeff each night to their house.

She had to admit that Jeff was stepping up to the plate. He'd been quick to help her out when she needed it. Dr. Hillyer had forbidden her to lift more than ten pounds or do anything requiring any serious exertion, and Tori had found she needed assistance to do something as simple as sitting up in bed. Even walking tired her out.

"It'll take your abdomen few weeks to recover," Sandra had consoled Tori in the hospital.

The day before she could bring Brendan home, the hospital had provided her with a private "going home" room for the night so that she could get used to being alone with Brendan before his discharge.

And now he was finally home.

Jeff pulled into the garage, and Tori saw the wheelchair ready. Jeff parked and came around to assist her.

As she'd been doing since her release, she leaned on his strong arm as he helped her from the car. She hated being dependent on him, yet somehow it felt right. She found his touch was as welcome as it was unwelcome. Touching him resurrected desire, reminding her that her body was as aware of his as it had been before Brendan's birth. Her skin heated, a sensation that offset the mid-November chill and left her longing for things off-limits if she planned on keeping her priorities straight.

Waiting in her wheelchair, she watched as Jeff reached inside the minivan and removed Brendan from his car seat, placing him in Tori's waiting arms. Tori held her son to her chest. "I'll get the stuff in the back later," Jeff said as he began to push her into the kitchen.

"Are you comfortable?" Jeff asked, pushing Tori into the great room.

"Fine," she said. Since that conversation in the NICU he'd done everything he could to please her. He'd spent the week at her side and not once had his phone rung or his pager beeped.

She'd found herself enjoying his company. There, in their own little niche of the noisy NICU, they had been isolated from the outside world. It was if they were a real family, but Tori hadn't dared to allow herself to believe that the feeling would last. For two years she'd been compartmentalized. While Jeff now had his entire focus on her and Brendan, she knew that reality and work would eventually intrude.

"I had wanted a quiet evening at home," Jeff told Tori as he helped her move from the wheelchair to the couch, "but my mother's patience has been exhausted and she won't wait another minute to see her grandson." He glanced at his phone. "My dad just sent a text message saying they've left the hotel and they're on their way over."

"Thanks, I'm sure it'll be fine," Tori said. "She's waited almost a week to see Brendan. And my parents have already seen him."

"True," Jeff said.

"So I'm sure your mom is ready. I would be." She smiled at him.

"Your parents are easier to handle," Jeff said.

"Maybe," Tori conceded. Her parents had visited her several times while she'd been in the maternity ward. Her mother had fallen in love on the spot with her first grandchild, and even Kenny had dubbed his nephew as being "all right for a pooping machine."

Now that Tori had her son home and he was doing so much better, she figured she could probably deal with the arrival of Rose Wright, especially since Jeff would be there. "Thank you," she said suddenly.

Jeff shifted and glanced at her. He seemed confused. "For what?"

"Just for everything you've done for me these past few weeks. You've been indispensable. You even found a pediatrician for Brendan when I'd not gotten around to that."

"It's nothing," Jeff said, waving off her praise.

"No, it isn't," Tori insisted. "You took care of me. Of us. That means a lot."

"I told you I would be here for you—" Jeff said, but if there was more he wanted to add, he didn't have a chance because the doorbell rang, and he went to answer it.

Rose stepped into the great room, dressed in a flowered shirt and black pants. Her husband, who looked uncannily like his sons, followed her. He was dressed casually in a collared shirt, a sweater and khakis.

"Mom," Jeff said, moving over to her and kissing her on the cheek. "Dad, come meet your grandson, Brendan."

"That's a good name. I do like it," Rose said. She studied the baby's face. "He's going to be a big, strong boy, just like you." She sat down next to Tori. "Congratulations, Mom. You did wonderful work. You should be very proud."

"Thanks," Tori said, blushing under the praise and from being called Mom. She adjusted Brendan's blanket. It was so strange to think of herself as a mother.

"He's beautiful," Rose said. "My twins were a little bit smaller. You must have been very scared."

"I was," Tori said. She'd also been slightly afraid that everyone would blame her for Brendan being premature. Tori chided herself for being so silly. Everyone had been nothing but supportive.

"If you'd be so kind, I'd love to hold my grandson," Rose said. "I'm way behind schedule here."

"Of course," Tori said, understanding Rose's impatience. Tori lifted Brendan and Rose's hands reached forward to take the sleeping boy. Rose settled herself against the back of the sofa and moved the swaddling cloth away from her grandson's face.

"He looks just like my twins did when they were born," she announced with evident pride. "Almost a mirror image." She turned to Tori and assessed her and the baby. "I can see some of you in his face, too. It's going to be fun watching this guy develop."

"Yeah, but it's another boy," Jeff said. "Disappointed?"

"Yes and no," Rose sighed, her disenchantment just for show. "You always promised me a girl and here I am, still surrounded by boys. Poor Hailey's the only granddaughter so far."

"Such a shame," Victor Wright teased. "Whatever will you do?"

The group settled in talking for a half hour before Rose let her husband hold the baby for a few minutes before taking Brendan again. After another ten minutes, Jeff's dad announced that it was probably past time to go.

Rose reluctantly handed the baby to Tori. "Since you didn't get an official baby shower, our family did a little shopping. You should find everything you need in the nursery and out in the garage. We'll pop in tomorrow to help you get everything sorted where you want it."

"You're too kind," Tori said, overwhelmed by their generosity.

"You're one of us now," Rose said, her tone matter of fact.

"But we're not married," Tori said.

"A mere technicality that I'm sure you'll eventually fix," Rose said. She leaned over and cooed at the baby. "You know, Brendan, you were just as bad as your daddy and uncle. They decided it was time to enter the world while I was at the movies. They didn't have rentals back then, either. Do you know I've never seen the end of that movie?"

Jeff's cell phone rang suddenly. He frowned as he read the number. "Excuse me a moment. I'll be right back."

He moved into the kitchen and returned soon after. "That was Justin," he told everyone. "Since I've taken the rest of this week and next off to work from home, Justin was just calling to say that he's got Darci and the new guy up to speed. He wanted me to tell Tori to do nothing, just relax and recuperate for the next eight weeks."

"That sounds like an excellent idea," Rose said. "All of it. Tori and the baby will need your help over the next few days. Besides, these are crucial bonding weeks for Brendan."

"I plan to be here for that," Jeff said. His gaze found Tori's and she flushed slightly. "I know my priorities."

Rose stood. "I never doubted your priorities for a minute," she said.

No, but Tori had, and that gentle dig was for her. Perhaps she'd deserved it, Tori thought later as, over the next week, Jeff remained true to his word and worked from home. He was there for the baby's two-week checkup, and after the doctor told them how well Brendan was doing, Jeff extended his time off for another week so that they had the week of Thanksgiving to themselves.

Each day Tori grew stronger. Her muscles had healed well enough that she could sit up on her own and walking was not as tiring as it once was.

Her body wasn't the only thing that had changed.

During the past three weeks she'd also seen a calmer, gentler Jeff, one more like the man she'd met so long ago, when she'd first started with Wright Solutions. Then they'd been pals, going out to dinner after work as just friends. She'd been a part of his life, not just someone to spend Saturday night with.

Even her mother commented on the change, noticing during Thanksgiving dinner how solicitous and careful he'd been with Tori and the baby. Her mother had patted Tori on the shoulder, her actions speaking volumes.

Admittedly, Tori liked that lately Jeff had been tender and gentle, paying attention to every detail. Even tonight he'd cooked a delicious dinner.

Speaking of food, it was time for Brendan's middle-of-the-night feeding. Tori had been awake for a few minutes and she rolled over and slowly swung her legs over the edge of her bed. Her feet found her slippers and she blinked as her eyes adjusted to the night-light's gentle glow. The clock flickered—two-fifteen. She went to the crib but, unlike previous nights, the baby was gone.

Except for one small lamp near the fireplace, the great room was dark as she approached it. But she could see the rhythmic movement of the rocking chair and hear the gentle thump of the wooden runners hitting the hardwood floor. An empty baby bottle sat on the floor.

"You were supposed to stay asleep," Jeff said before she'd even stepped into his peripheral vision. "You need your rest, Tori. Brendan ate a good three ounces and went right back down."

"I can see that," Tori said. Her throat constricted slightly as she looked over Jeff's shoulder.

Was there any more beautiful or peaceful sight than this? Brendan lay against Jeff's bare stomach, safe and secure in his father's arms. Her baby had grown; his beautiful lips puckered as he slept, enjoying what appeared to be sweet dreams. One of his little fists rested safely on his father's much larger palm.

Jeff stopped rocking. "What time is it?"

"About twenty minutes past two," she said. "It's late. You're working tomorrow. I would have gotten him."

"I thought you could use the break. I didn't mind. I can handle it."

She moved forward. "What, getting up?"

He yawned. "Yeah. That. Although, I admit I've been a bit spoiled staying home. As much as I don't want to, since December's just days away, I'll have to start going into the office. However, tomorrow shouldn't be too busy and I'll be back before you know it. I have been proving that I've been around, haven't I?"

"You have," Tori said as she leaned over to take her son from his arms. "It's been wonderful having you here. I'll miss you."

"Will you?"

"I will," Tori answered. "But don't worry about us— Brendan and I will be fine. I'm doing pretty well and I'm halfway through my recovery."

She took Brendan, who simply stretched and shifted slightly as he moved from his father's arms into his mother's. Holding her son close, she delighted in the soft, sweet-smelling bundle of life she'd created and loved. She noticed that Jeff had even changed Brendan's diaper.

Jeff followed Tori back into the bedroom and Tori set Brendan down in the crib, placing him securely on his back. She kept him wrapped in the receiving blankets and covered him with another.

"He's perfect, you know," Jeff whispered, his voice filled with wonder. "So absolutely perfect. You and I did a fantastic thing. Thank you."

"You're welcome," she managed to say as guilt roared in and caused tears to fall. Watching Jeff these past two weeks, she'd contemplated a dozen or more times every single word she'd said about him not being a good father. He'd certainly proved her wrong. He loved their son. He was a great father.

As for their own relationship, even though things were better between them, she doubted Jeff would ever care for her in the way she truly wanted. Her hormones were still out of control and a small sniffle escaped as she tried to hide the tears that streamed down her face.

Jeff touched her shoulder. "Tori, what's wrong?"

"It's..." She stopped. What could she say? What words would make the situation right? She'd vowed not to let love come into this "relationship" and was kicking herself for wanting it more than ever. Staying with Jeff was what was best for Brendan, at least that's what she'd always thought. But she couldn't blurt out that she was falling for him again only to be rejected once more.

Jeff's strong fingers began kneading her shoulders,

trying to loosen her muscles. "You're too tense," he said. "Relax so when you can climb back into bed you can fall right to sleep. Don't worry. I've got you. Let go of the stress."

Tori let her head fall forward as Jeff's fingers worked their magic. His gentle yet insistent touch traveled up her neck and over her head. He slid his hand down her neck and over her shoulders. She leaned into him, letting his strong body support hers.

"That's better," he whispered, his breath warm against her ear. "Let that tension go. See? Everything's fine. I'm here. I'm not going anywhere."

He was there, physically. Through the thinness of her nightdress, Tori could feel Jeff's presence behind her. She sensed the moment his caress began providing pleasure and felt the hardness of his arousal as it pressed into her back.

It would be so easy to surrender to his desire, and let him slake himself deep inside her as he'd done so many times before. Tori knew that they could easily step down that path again.

As much as she wanted to deny it, having him truly love her mattered. She knew she'd never stopped loving him. She couldn't stop loving him, even when she'd tried to separate herself from him. Nothing she did could shut him out. In the end, she still wanted him and wanted to be with him. She lived in his house. She worked at his company. He was devoted to her, yes, yet her love was as deep and unrequited as it had ever been and she had to accept that.

More tears threatened to fall; Tori needed to escape his touch. She tried to step away from him, but the bassinet was directly in front of her and to move to her bed she had to turn and face him.

When she did, her step faltered. Up close Jeff cut an impressive figure. She longed to trace those kissable lips with her fingertips. Somehow, she managed to find her voice. "I—I should go back to sleep. Brendan will be up in another three hours and you have to go in to work."

The glow of the night-light added mystery and shadows to his face, but even those failed to hide the need and desire clearly evident. His body blocked her way to her bed. The husky words that came from deep inside him sent an illicit thrill through her.

"Do you know how beautiful you are?" he asked. "You're a siren…"

His hand reached forward as if of its own volition, snaking gently into Tori's hair. Inch by inch his face drew nearer—that handsome, perfect face on which Tori had once planted endless kisses. Closer came his smooth skin, the round chin, the slightly crooked nose and those lips that could kiss ever so gently or wildly with unrestrained passion.

The last thing she saw were his fathomless green eyes as his mouth claimed hers.

Immediately, the embers of the fire that always threatened to consume them flared to life once again. This was where they connected, where for a moment she could pretend that he loved her as they reached another plane.

The desire that burned between them gave legitimacy to repressed need as Tori's and Jeff's lips molded together as if both were afraid something could douse the fire they were creating.

As he plundered her mouth a wash of pure desire thundered through her body, sending pools of heat to her curled toes. Her arms slid up his chest and she cupped his face. The night's beard growth gently prickled and teased her fingertips as they stroked his cheeks.

His mouth demanded hers and Tori swayed into him, her need as evident as his. The kiss deepened. Then suddenly it was ending as he withdrew his lips and stepped away from her. A wash of cold chillier than a frigid shower immediately descended around Tori's heart.

He swore at himself. She stepped forward, but he held up his hands. The movement indicated she should stay where she was. "I'm sorry," he said.

He shook his head savagely. "You just had major surgery," he said, berating himself. "I shouldn't have touched you. I could have hurt you. I never want to hurt you."

"Jeff, it's all right. Seriously. We live together. We can have both the passion and the friendship. There's nothing wrong with a kiss now and then. I liked it. To make this situation between us work, all the pieces have to be there."

They had to be. She didn't want him keeping her compartmentalized any longer. To continually reject her sexually hurt. They had to find a common thread aside from their baby.

Jeff shook his head. "I don't want to mess up any more. You want more than sex, Tori. So do I, until you believe just how much I care for you, that I can love you, I don't want to push you into anything. I couldn't forgive myself if I did."

Still angry with himself, he stepped way from her. "Get some rest. As you said, Brendan will be up soon and you need your sleep."

"Okay," Tori said, watching him stride from the room. She climbed into bed and pressed a finger to her still-tingling lips. He'd kissed her and left her.

What did he mean by not being able to forgive himself? Did he mean because he couldn't love her? She forced herself to close her eyes as myriad thoughts bounced around inside her head like a dozen ping-pong balls. Maybe his emotions ran deeper than she'd suspected. Whatever was going on, they couldn't go backward. They had to get through this.

Chapter Fourteen

He'd kissed Tori! Jeff pushed aside the bowl of half-eaten cereal. He couldn't eat another bite. He had no appetite this morning and had had even less sleep.

Kissing Tori had been like a flash fire or a dormant volcano erupting unannounced after a long absence. The intensity of last night's kiss had shaken him to his very core.

He resisted the urge to bang his fist on the kitchen table. Just one touch and he'd lost all rational thought. He'd forgotten to exercise any restraint, having been swept away on a current of pure emotion.

He'd wanted to woo her, not seduce her. Kissing Tori last night had been beyond the ordinary desire he'd felt before. Jeff had tossed and turned all night.

He and Tori had become closer emotionally—beyond anything he'd felt for her during their earlier friendship. He didn't want to lose that. He loved her.

He only wanted her to be happy. He'd always been the one to maintain the parameters of their relationship and now, for the first time, he'd seen full consequences of his actions.

He'd kept Tori at arm's length these past few years

because she was the one. Last night's kiss had shown him that she had claimed his heart.

Maybe he had had another one of those "aha" light-bulb moments last night, for this morning he knew without a doubt that she was not only the one he loved, but his other half, probably the better half. Not being the Casanova Justin was, Jeff had always distanced himself where women were concerned, dating here and there, no one capturing permanent interest. Until Tori. Hindsight showed him she'd been right in saying he kept her compartmentalized. In the beginning, he'd been afraid she might leave him again, as she'd done that first week. He'd likely been deeply in love with her then, although he'd never been in love and didn't recognize that was how he'd felt. Maybe that's why he'd chased her, yet still held back from giving himself to her completely.

Love was a two-sided coin. It could be wonderful and blinding, but flip it over and the person could hurt you faster than a knife. If Tori was his life mate, that meant she was also the one with the power to deteriorate the *vrahas,* the rock, and turn it into useless sand.

She was the woman he loved, although love was an elusive concept he'd never understood. Because he'd been so cautious, he'd never had his heart broken as Justin or Jared had, and Jeff had been afraid to open to Tori and risk getting hurt.

And now, even if he told her how he felt, he was down on the count and she might not believe him. He'd seen her skepticism every day he'd remained home from work. She'd wondered, when the phone rang, if he'd jump up and rush to the office. No matter what he did, no matter how many times he proved himself worthy, he'd already done so much irreparable damage over the past two years. How did one get past that? He had no answers.

"Good morning." Tori appeared in the kitchen, a peaceful bundle nestled in her arms. Jeff found his orange juice powdering in his mouth.

She appeared ethereal. Her dark brown hair had grown and hung loose, barely skimming her shoulders, the strands caressing the skin his fingers had touched the night before. Her white robe covered her rounded mother's body, hiding from his sight her full, lush curves; curves he still longed for.

In an attempt to control his desire, he dropped his attention to her feet. She'd never been much of a slipper person and this morning her feet were bare. She looked like a nymph bringing her offering to the gods as she leaned over to show him Brendan, who gurgled when he saw his father.

"Good morning," he managed to answer, not surprised at all to hear his voice sound a little gruff. "Are you hungry? Do you want something to eat?"

"You finish your food. I'll get it," she said. She walked forward, her feet padding on the linoleum. She placed Brendan in his bouncy seat, strapped him in tight and set him on the floor. Buddy the cat strolled over, sniffed the baby and moved on, Brendan's eyes trying to track the animal as it walked away.

Jeff turned his attention to Tori. She seemed tired, as if she'd spent a restless night, as well. "How did you sleep?" he asked, concerned. The last thing he wanted was for her to push herself.

"Not well," she admitted.

"If I disturbed you when I got up, I'm sorry," Jeff said.

"Actually…" Tori fixed a bottle for Brendan. Be-

cause of the pain medication she was taking for the
C-section, she'd opted not to breast-feed. "You've never
kissed me like that before, and then as fast as you
started, you stopped. I was wondering why."

"I was wrong in kissing you like that," Jeff said, a
pounding beginning behind his left eyebrow.

Her hand hovered over the formula. A little powder
spilled from the plastic scoop onto the countertop.
"What do you mean, you were wrong in kissing me?"

He was already botching this. How could he explain
he didn't want the sex thing clouding his feelings? He'd
failed to express that last night. Also, one didn't just
blurt out I love you, did they?

"I don't break, Jeff," she said, her brown eyes widen-
ing in surprise. "I'm recovering well. Better than expected, actually. Brendan is doing great. It's okay to
want me. That's normal."

"That's not it," he said. He did want her. Too much.
He loved her. Maybe you were just supposed to blurt
out the words and…

He knew he'd bungled his answer and paused too
long when Tori said, "Don't you want me?" She
frowned. He'd meant to apologize for rushing her, but
instead he'd wounded her pride.

He was constantly doing something wrong. He'd
been wrong to box her in. Wrong to badger her to marry
him when he'd first learned she was expecting. Wrong
in the way he was handling this conversation. Despite
his newfound insight and feelings, maybe he'd been
wanting to coerce something that simply couldn't be.

He had no idea. Emotions weren't linear and troubles
related to them weren't easily solved. He was terrible
with this aspect of his life. Jeff liked problems to be

straightforward, which is why he preferred computers and math equations. No matter how complex the work he needed to do was, he was in control. He was making too many mistakes with Tori, doing more damage than good. No wonder he'd tossed and turned all night.

She placed her hands on her hips, the formula forgotten. Brendan was content staring at the cat. "Do you want me, Jeff?" she repeated.

He wanted to stop hurting her. He wanted her to be happy. He wanted what was best for everyone and right now he wasn't sure what that was. His emotions were zinging inside his brain and giving him a headache; he never had headaches. He struggled for a generic answer that wouldn't deteriorate the situation any further. "Your doctor has outlawed any sex until after your mandatory eight-week recovery period," he said, sidestepping the question.

"Yes, she has, but that doesn't mean you can't kiss me," Tori said. "I'm not a fragile china doll. We can still kiss and do…a few other things. I enjoyed being with you last night. I've missed your touch. If we're going to make this relationship work, we have to connect."

And wasn't that the problem? Jeff thought. The only place they'd ever felt connected before had been in bed. He couldn't risk going back to that. The physical. She'd left him because that's all the relationship had been.

Last night's kiss had shown him the passion between them hadn't disappeared. Jeff was afraid if they gave in to their desires, he'd lose everything he'd been working toward. He didn't want Tori to feel she'd settled. He wanted her to love him again.

His cell phone began to trill. "I'm sorry. Can you hold on for a minute?" he asked. He retrieved the phone from his pants pocket and answered the call. "Jeff Wright."

While Jeff listened, out of the corner of his eye, he watched Tori finish preparing the baby's formula. "Now's not a good time for this," he said. "I'm right in the middle of something."

Tori lifted Brendan from his seat, cradled him in her arms and brought the bottle to his lips. She sat down in the chair across from Jeff, her son sucking down his breakfast enthusiastically. She arched her eyebrow at Jeff in question.

Jeff grimaced as he continued to listen to the caller, one of Wright Solutions' first-responders. The situation Dave described was desperate and, as much as Jeff didn't like the situation, he knew he was going to have to be on-site—the crew was making little headway. This was his area of expertise and they had waited until they'd exhausted all avenues before calling him.

"Let me grab a suitcase and I'll be on my way," he finally told the man. "I'll meet you there. No, don't worry. I'll rent a car at the airport."

"Let me guess—work crisis," Tori said when Jeff ended the call.

"Huge work crisis," Jeff replied. "Started last night and our team still can't find the problem. They get the system back online and it's down again within five minutes. Since I wrote the programming, they need me in Denver to fix whatever's going on."

"What's going on?" Tori asked, as Jeff had told her the name of the company.

"They got hit by lightning in those storms that crossed the Rockies the other night. The building took not only a power surge but they lost power for almost five hours. We can't get anything to run properly without shutting down and their tech guys are having difficulty recovering three weeks of data from the back-ups. I've got to take this. I'll be headed out within a few minutes."

"When will you be back?" Tori asked. Brendan had finished eating and she put him on her shoulder, gently patting his back to make him burp.

Jeff shook his head, not sure how long it would take him to get things right. "I'll call once I get there and keep you updated. I'll be back as soon as I can, I promise. You and I have a conversation to finish."

He rose to his feet and stood there awkwardly. In all the times Jeff had left for business trips, he'd never kissed her goodbye. Maybe he should change that. How should he start? Just plant his lips on hers?

He moved over to her, staring down at Brendan who was now reclining in his mother's arms, his eyes closed. He slept so peacefully. "I've got to pack," Jeff said lamely.

"I know," Tori said.

"If it wasn't work, I wouldn't be going," Jeff continued. "I've made some decisions. I want to tell you some things. We'll talk the minute I get back."

"I understand," she said.

Jeff stood there awkwardly, then leaned to kiss her on the forehead before moving away. He felt Tori's gaze on him as he left the kitchen. God, don't let him have blown it. He loved her. He didn't want them to be two roommates playing house for the rest of his life.

For a man who solved problems and crisis after crisis

for a living, Jeff prayed that he could figure this one out. His future depended on it. If he failed, he was going to lose everything that really mattered. Tori. Brendan. And a major piece of himself.

Chapter Fifteen

"Surprise!"

When Tori opened the door at five o'clock Saturday evening, her jaw dropped open at the scene greeting her on her doorstep. She could only see Joann, but as her friend moved aside, she saw Lisa and Cecile standing right behind her. Tori blinked to make sure the image wasn't an illusion. "Oh my God! What are you all doing here?"

"Surprising you," Cecile said as she stomped her feet on the doormat. "Hurry up and let us in. It's cold outside."

"Yes, yes, sorry. Get in here. I just can't believe you're here." Tori admitted her friends, then quickly closed the door, shutting out the December wind. Missouri hadn't yet received any snow although Christmas was twenty-something days away.

"I told you yesterday on the phone that I'd take care of you," Joann said, reaching to give Tori a big hug before placing her purse on a side table. "What you didn't know when we talked was that I was already in Kansas City and that I'd called these two Thursday night and we planned this."

"You kept a secret from me?" Tori said.

Lisa grinned. "We did. Quite a good one, too, if I do say so myself. And we pulled it off because here we are and you still have a dazed expression. We didn't want you to be alone on your birthday. Okay, we missed it by a few days, but we're here. You told Joann that Jeff still wasn't back and probably won't be back until Monday."

Tori shook her head. "Yes, he's still in Denver. The situation is a lot more complicated than it first appeared to be and there's no way he can leave. They've been working nonstop."

"Like you used to do," Lisa said.

"I know. Seems like such a long time ago and I have to admit I don't miss it a bit. Gosh, where are my manners? Let me take your coats."

"Not yet. We still have to go back outside," Joann said. "We decided you needed an official baby shower and birthday party, so we've got all sorts of bags filled with goodies in the car. We went shopping today. Thirty is a big deal."

"You shouldn't have," Tori said, already overwhelmed. With all the chaos of Brendan's arrival and Jeff's departure, her birthday had been the last thing on her mind.

"Yes, we should," Cecile added. "We had a great time and you're going to reap the benefits. So we're going to run out and get everything and you're going to let us. Where should we put it?"

"The great room," Tori decided. "We'll settle ourselves in there."

"Awesome. I like this house. By the way, you're giving us a tour. Right after we see the baby," Lisa proclaimed and, twenty minutes later, after unloading everything and oohing and ahhing over Brendan in his crib, her friends got cozy on the couches, a ton of wrapped presents resting at Tori's feet.

"I still can't believe you did all this," Tori said in awe. She'd thought she'd be spending Saturday night alone, and then, all of the sudden, here were her very best friends. "I can't believe you guys managed to organize this."

"It was pretty easy," Joann said, smiling. "I drove up from Springfield, Missouri, and met Cecile at the airport."

"I hopped on the train," Lisa said. "Amazingly, I had some free time since my boss doesn't officially become governor until January and he and his wife are taking a much-needed four-day vacation in Antigua. A belated anniversary trip to the beach."

"Oh, don't mention warmth," Cecile said. "Chicago's already got snow, so I'm ready to stop sliding in the slush. What was I thinking, returning to the downtown and its lake effect?"

"Gee, I don't know? Hot man? New job?" Tori teased.

"Yeah, okay," Cecile said. "But this gave me an excuse to go somewhere drier."

Cecile twirled her wineglass before taking a sip and gesturing to the group. "We're all together to celebrate again."

Yes, they were, Tori thought. Not only had her friends come bearing gifts, but they'd also shown up with a bottle of wine and a meat, cheese and cracker tray to go with it. Since Joann wasn't due till March, she was having water, but Tori could indulge a little.

"So, open something," Cecile said. "I'm dying to see what you think, especially since we had so much fun picking things out."

"Great, that's pressure," Tori said with a laugh. "What if I hate it?"

"We'll give you the receipt and you can brave the holiday throng. Start with that pile on your right. That's the baby stuff," Lisa said.

Tori opened the presents, finding everything from diapers to the cutest little-boy clothes. Then she turned her attention to the gifts stacked to her left. These were more intimate items—scented candles, bubble bath, body lotion and…Tori held up a garment made of sheer lace. "You guys bought me lingerie?"

"Absolutely," Cecile said. "Got to keep that spark alive. Luke loves it when I wear the stuff."

"No details," Tori shrieked. She sobered. "Besides, sex is off-limits until almost New Year's. Not that Jeff…" Her face clouded and before she could hide her sad expression, everyone noticed.

"What is it?" Cecile demanded.

"I'm not really sure," Tori admitted. "I wish I knew."

She told them about the kiss and the conversation the morning after. "It's like all those rumors I heard from the married girls at the office. You know, the ones who have been hitched for about ten years. They have no sex life, or at least it's very infrequent."

"I have quite a good sex life," Joann said, "and I have three kids and this one on the way." She patted her stomach. "You can't listen to the naysayers. You just have to get creative with your, um, locations and timing."

"Creativity isn't the problem. Jeff always wanted me. All he has to do is touch me and I'd want him. Yet now…"

"Sweetie, you're still healing," Joann said. "He was probably worried. He's a guy. They're stupid about these things. Even Kyle was petrified of harming me. Treated me like glass."

"Yes, but he won't even kiss me," Tori said. "How are we going to make this work if he won't kiss me anymore?"

"Does he know how you feel about him?" Joann asked.

Tori blinked. "What do you mean?"

"Does he know you love him?" Joann asked. "We—" she paused and indicated the other Roses "—were talking over dinner yesterday. We know you love him, but does he know you love him? I mean, have you told him? You two are the worst communicators of any couple we know, but that doesn't mean you can't work on that aspect and get everything out in the open."

"I agreed to move in with him," Tori said stubbornly.

"Yes, but not because you wanted to be with him. Brendan arrived early and helped you with that decision."

"Yeah, but what if I tell him I love him and, like last time, he says he needs his space and that he doesn't want the relationship to go in that direction? I'd rather not go through that again. I'd rather live without."

"Never," Lisa said. "And how do you know he doesn't love you? Look at all he's done. He probably hasn't said the words. You have to stop thinking in old patterns. Nothing kills a relationship faster."

"Maybe Jeff's still sorting things out," Joann added. "Just because he cut off the kiss doesn't mean he doesn't want you. Never doubt that, sweetie. He's probably never stopped wanting you. But now, things have changed. That's scary, especially for men. They aren't good with change."

"Are you sure?" Tori asked.

Joann nodded. "He's probably going crazy. You've mentioned that he's always been laid back, but I'm guessing that all this has shown him that he's not as un-affected by life as he thought he was. I think he's had a huge wake-up call with all of this."

Tori thought about that for a moment. Jeff had seemed as though he were walking on eggshells lately.

"Maybe," she said. "We've always been very physical and now we tiptoe around each other. He's trying to be the perfect guy. He's done everything he said he'd do. It's almost like he's trying too hard."

"Maybe he is," Cecile said. "That's good, isn't it?"

"I think he's afraid of losing you," Joann said.

Doubtful, Tori stared at Joann, but both Lisa and Cecile were nodding in agreement. "How can he be afraid of losing me?"

"He just is," Lisa said.

"I don't understand." Tori shook her head. Jeff wasn't a guy who got upset often. He didn't love her. What did he have to lose?

Joann took a sip of her water. "He may not even recognize his feelings himself, but you're the mother of his child. He's come after you twice. He might not understand why he did that, but I think I do. Deep down, he loves you. That means you have the power to hurt him. You've always told us that he's not great with women."

"No, he's not. Never was," Tori said.

"So, put yourself in his shoes. You two work together. The minute you break up with your boyfriend, he's there to pick up the pieces and you have a night of great sex. Then, the morning after, you say it's a mistake and go back to the other guy."

Tori nodded. "Yes, that was after the Christmas party."

"Is there another one this year?" Lisa interjected.

"Yes, this weekend in St. Louis. I guess it's on right

now. We weren't planning to go, even without Jeff being out of town. Brendan's doing well, but I still feel it's too soon to travel. Everyone's going to come here for the holidays before they head down to Branson anyway. Rose insisted on it."

Cecile coughed. "Anyway," she prodded.

Joann began again. "You and Jeff worked things out in the end and started dating, or whatever it was."

"Sex," Tori said.

"We know. Then you get into a routine and life's well."

"Only for a while. He didn't love me," Tori said. "I told him I wanted more and he didn't. I had two choices. Accept it or leave him. I did both."

"Which brings us to now. Things have changed. Maybe he does love you," Joann added.

"He and I have talked about it. He's never denied or confirmed his feelings," Tori said. "He simply stares at me."

"You never mentioned that. How long ago was this?" Cecile asked.

Tori frowned. "August? Lisa's wedding? I don't remember."

"Still, that was months ago," Lisa said.

Joann leaned forward. "Men are like onions. Layer after layer of stuff that is designed to make your eyes water, until you get to the center. Think back over these past four months. How have they been?"

"They've been…nice. Almost like he's trying too hard to please me. So, see, I'm back to that." Tori sighed.

"But you have your answer. He's trying," Joann said.

Brendan's cry came through the baby monitor and Tori rose. "I'll be right back," she said.

"Men are like onions?" Tori heard Cecile say to Joann as Tori left the room. "Where do you get this stuff?"

"I thought it was brilliant," Joann said.

Tori smiled as she listened to her friends. Their surprise arrival had been a pick-me-up, even if they'd begun to analyze her and Jeff's relationship.

Tori retrieved Brendan from his bassinet. She took a moment to glance at the bed, the same one she and Jeff had slept in long ago in his St. Louis condo.

She had to do something to change the situation. The phone rang and she grabbed it from the bedside table, cradling the receiver to her ear with her shoulder as she changed Brendan's diaper. "Hello?"

"Hey." It was Jeff. "I have a quick break before going back to this all-nighter and I wanted to give you a call. Justin called today. When I'm done with this, I need to go to St. Louis for a meeting. Then he's promised I can come home and won't have to travel like this ever again."

"Okay," Tori said.

"I wish I were there with you," he said.

"Joann, Lisa and Cecile are here," Tori said, not responding to his words. "They surprised me with a baby shower and birthday party. I didn't know they were coming tonight."

"Neither did I, but that's wonderful," Jeff said. "I assume you guys are having a great chat."

"Cecile told us all about her wedding. She's planning on getting married next June when the show she works on is on hiatus for a month."

"That sounds good," Jeff said. His call-waiting beeped. "Hold on," he said as he switched to the other line. Tori used the opportunity to bring Brendan out into the great room. Lisa gladly held him while Tori went into the kitchen and prepared some formula, the phone still lodged between her shoulder and her ear.

Jeff clicked over a few minutes later. "That was one of the guys. I'm going to have to cut this short. As soon as I have the meeting, I'll be home that night. No later than Friday. Tori…" he said, pausing.

"Yes?" she asked.

"I'm sorry for having put you through what I did. We'll talk when I get home, okay?"

"Okay," she said, her fingers gripping the formula bottle.

"So I'll see you on or before this weekend." With that, Jeff disconnected.

Tori set the cordless phone down on the counter and walked back out into the great room. She handed the bottle to Lisa, who popped the nipple into Brendan's mouth.

"Tori, you look like you've seen a ghost," Cecile said.

"I have. I think he's going to leave me." She relayed the conversation. "He's going to let me go."

Her friends stared at her. "Then the question is do you want to let him go?" Joann said.

"I thought that was what I wanted last April. Even now I know I can't live like this forever. Something has to change."

"It's been changing all along," Lisa said. "With or without your approval or notice."

"But if he doesn't love me, what else can be different but our living arrangements? He wants me to be happy."

"He's working off old information," Joann said. "You haven't given him anything new to work with."

"Maybe it's time for a detour. Take matters into your own hands," Lisa said.

"How?" It sounded perfect—and absolutely frightening. "What am I supposed to do?"

"What do you really want?" Lisa asked. "You've got to decide. It's going to be a risk either way."

"I'm not sure." Tori's lip trembled. She loved Jeff. Always had. Always would. "I want it all. Love. Tenderness. Like the vows you guys read at your weddings. But how do I get him to tell me he loves me? How do I make him reach out?"

"Well, you go for it," Cecile said. "You grab what you want, and that's Jeff. You're not going to let him go, are you?"

"No," Tori said. "No, I'm not letting him out of my life."

"That's the spirit I haven't seen in a while," Lisa said. In her arms, Brendan ate on, content.

"Thank goodness tomorrow is Sunday," Joann said. "You need a plan and I have a feeling this is going to take all night."

"Whatever it takes," Tori said. "I'm ready. I have my baby and I want his father. He's not leaving me. Ever."

"Then let's get to work."

Chapter Sixteen

"So how's Tori doing?" Justin asked during a lull in the business meeting, a plate of carrot sticks and dip in his hand. "Lauren's insisting I eat healthier," he said, indicating his meal, but Jeff hadn't really been paying attention to the food his twin was eating.

Instead he was contemplating what he'd do tonight when he'd finally be home. He'd been gone too long and travel didn't hold the same appeal. If his brothers hadn't needed him, he would have flown home the moment the Denver job finished, instead of being in St. Louis at a working buffet luncheon.

"Tori's fine," Jeff said. "Her friends came to visit her this past weekend, so she wasn't alone. They popped in for a surprise baby shower. She said they gave her tons of presents."

"I guess I meant, how are you and Tori doing?" Justin clarified. He reached for the bottle of water he'd set on the sidebar.

"We're fine," Jeff said. He dangled his own water bottle from his fingertips. "I gave her a birthday gift and she said she liked it."

Justin shook his head. "You aren't fine. You're a

mess and you look like hell," he proclaimed flatly. "If I'd known you were going to look this bad I'd have sent you home. You'll scare our future clients. What happened between you two?"

Jeff sighed. Maybe he should confide in Justin, after all they'd been sharing things since the womb.

"I feel as if I'm screwing everything up. Daily," he said. "I feel like I've put way too much pressure on her and now she's settling for me. It's as if she's giving up on us just when I'm starting to fight. I only want her to be happy."

"Have you talked to her about this?" Justin asked between bites.

"I told her we'd talk tonight when I get back," Jeff said. "I told her we had to change this."

"That's a given. Let me ask you this. Do you miss her?" Justin asked.

"Yes." Jeff frowned. "I've called her every night. I've made sure to e-mail her. Of course I miss her. What kind of a question is that?"

"An important one," Justin said. "When I'm away from Lauren I feel as if a part of me is gone. Now that we're married it's not as devastating, but rather an odd sense of comfort. It tells me that, you know what, I care for her a great deal. I love my wife. She's everything to me. I'm still whole, but I'm ready to return home the minute I leave. That's love. I never want to lose her. You're the same way about Tori except that you've been too dense to realize it."

"I'm not dense," Jeff said, because pride meant he had to defend himself, at least, to his brother. In all honesty, though, Jeff knew Justin was right.

Justin saw right through the smoke screen. "Yes, you are. I know you. You don't want to dig inside yourself because you're afraid that the deeper you go, the greater the risk becomes. You've only loved one person, and that's Tori. Me, I thought I was in love a bunch of times before Lauren. Then I realized I'd found the real thing. You're the opposite. You found the real thing the first time."

"Maybe," Jeff said.

"You love her. Admit it to yourself so that both of you have a chance."

Jeff lifted the water to his lips, giving him a few seconds of thinking time. He took a long swallow. "I do love her," he admitted. Saying the words aloud for the first time sealed his emotions. "But she'd never believe me if I just blurted it out. I've made so many mistakes. This is complicated. More so than it was with you and Lauren. That was just a simple misunderstanding."

"No, that was me being stubborn and failing to trust or believe my feelings. You don't know what Tori will do or how she'll react to your declaration because you've given yourself excuse after excuse not to find out how she really feels. Tell her you love her. That's what she wants. If she doesn't believe you, hang on. The ride might get bumpy, but it will end in the right place. Eventually she'll stop running. Now go home and talk to Tori. Tell her how you feel."

"I was already planning on it," Jeff said, knowing Justin was correct. Deep inside his soul, Jeff didn't want to let Tori go. He didn't want to leave her, or to have her leave him. He wanted her happy, but he wanted that happiness to be with him. He wanted his family. He'd start by telling Tori he loved her.

AND HE DID LOVE HER. But when he arrived home on Friday, he found Tori exhausted from a trying day dealing with Brendan, so Jeff had taken over baby duty.

He'd helped out, enjoying the time with his son. Tori went to bed early and Jeff stayed up late watching TV.

Saturday he rose later than he'd intended, around ten. He got up, but as soon as he entered the kitchen to speak with her, she'd left the baby in his arms and gone grocery and Christmas shopping.

When the phone rang about four o'clock, he picked it up, only to find Justin on the line.

"I haven't heard from you and I'm dying to know what's going on," his brother said. "Is everything better in your neck of the woods?"

"No," Jeff admitted. "We haven't talked. Right now she's out shopping. Tonight we'll talk."

He heard the garage door and said, "She's home. I'll talk to you later."

Tori came in, carrying multiple grocery bags.

"Let me help," Jeff said.

"I've got it," she said.

"No, you don't." Jeff reached for the plastic bags and saw they contained steaks. "Tori, what is going on?"

"I'm surprising you," Tori said. "I'm going to cook dinner. Now I have to get the rest of the bags before things spoil."

"Tori, you're not doing anything until you tell me what's going on. I feel like you're shutting me out." He reached out and touched her arm.

"We will talk," she said. "But we're having dinner first. Will you please just let me play this my way?"

The way she asked resonated within him. "Okay," he said. "I'll do it your way."

Her pretty brown eyes widened. "Dinner will be at six," she told him.

Jeff headed up to his bedroom and phoned his brother back. "She's cooking me dinner."

"Maybe this is her grand gesture to you," Justin said. "Whatever the outcome, let her make it. Just remember to hold on if necessary."

Great, Jeff thought as he closed his phone, ending the call.

The doorbell rang and Tori called, "Can you get that please?"

Jeff went back downstairs only to face a delivery-man. "Last one of the day," he said. "Your wife is very persuasive. Where do you want me to set this grill?"

The man wheeled in a large box containing what looked to be a very expensive charcoal barbecue pit. "Uh, the screened-in porch," Jeff said. Tori was barbe-cuing? It was the middle of December. If they wanted steak, they could go out to eat. Brendan had gone to several restaurants already, sleeping the events away.

Jeff let the man in to the porch, shut the door behind him and strode to the kitchen. Tori was in the middle of putting groceries away.

"Hey," he said gently. The last thing he needed was for her to bolt. "I guess you got me an early Christmas present."

"I did," she said. She raised her chin and stared at him, her expression hopeful. "I wanted to do something special for you. I'm going to make a special dinner and…"

Jeff gazed at her, loving her gesture but not wanting her to do it for all the wrong reasons. "Tori, I think we need to talk about us and clear the air first."

"Talk first?" Tori repeated, wanting to make certain

she'd heard him correctly. She'd planned on doing that afterward. She was going to make his favorite foods, wine him and dine him a little. Then, when the mood and moment were right, she'd tell him she loved him and let him know what she hoped their future could be like.

But when Jeff shook his head, she knew he wasn't going to let her continue until they talked. He took a deep breath.

"Tori, we always seem to say the wrong things so I'm praying this comes out right. I'm releasing you. I don't want you to stay with me because this is how I wanted things months ago. I want you in my life, but I don't want you to feel like you're settling."

"Oh God, I was right," she said. "You're leaving me."

"Leaving you?"

Jeff took her hand, the ever-present sizzle zinging between them. She closed her eyes in defeat, but the darkness didn't bring solace.

"I'm not going anywhere. Don't shut me out," he said.

"Shut you out?" Her eyes flashed open as anger took root. "What have you done for two years? You never loved me. You never even bothered to try."

"No, I didn't," Jeff admitted. "I was selfish. I only wanted what was best and easiest for me. I wanted things between us to be simple. You were the first woman who ever lasted more than a few dates. I've never been serious about anyone and the idea of being serious scared me. When I told you I didn't want more, you went along with it and I was comfortable with that. Smack me if you want, I deserve it. I liked that you fit me and I took advantage of that."

"I tried to leave you so many times," she said.

"I realize that now," Jeff said. "You ran the very first time and it petrified me. I didn't want to be like your ex who said he loved you and then didn't. I loved you and never told you, but that wasn't the answer either. No wonder you left. I deserved that.

"When I first confronted you about being pregnant and asked you to marry me, you were right to turn me down. You nailed me perfectly when you said I didn't consider your needs. Well, I'm considering them now. You shouldn't have to settle for me, Tori, if I'm not the man you want. You deserve a future with the man of your choice. So don't do this because you think I want it. Not if it means you giving up a part of yourself."

Silence fell in the kitchen as Jeff's final statement replayed itself over and over in her head.

"So where do we go from here?" she asked.

"I'm not really sure," Jeff said. "I've never been in this spot before and I'm afraid of making more mistakes. I don't want to hurt you, Tori. That's the last thing I've ever wanted and I've been doing that since the very beginning of our relationship. I never should have pursued you. You were vulnerable when we first got together and I couldn't help myself. I'd liked you for so long and when the chance came, I took it. I was selfish."

"No, you weren't. I'd liked you for quite a long time, too," she admitted. "I had had the biggest crush on you from the very first minute we met. I was afraid that what we'd shared was one-sided, though. And I'd had a lot to drink."

"And I took advantage," Jeff said. "But even after we got together, I didn't take our relationship to the next level. Just because we were monogamous didn't mean we were good together."

"No, it didn't," Tori admitted. "I wanted you to fall in love with me, but it seemed more and more hopeless, especially after you told me that you didn't want more. I knew the only one who could change was me."

Jeff raked a hand through his hair. "If I tell you that I love you, will you believe me?" he asked.

"You love me?" she asked, her heart leaping at his question.

"Yeah, I do," Jeff said. "I think I always have. But I'd never been in love before, so I didn't really know what I was feeling. Love scares me. I like things simple and straightforward—emotions are like a foreign language I don't speak. The day you had Brendan was like being hit on the head with a two-by-four. I'd already been trying to woo you, but at that moment I realized how much of an idiot I'd been all along. I was doing it for the wrong reasons. I hadn't admitted to myself the depth of what I felt for you."

"You never have," Tori said.

"I have now," Jeff said. "But by then I'd created a huge mess. If I told you how much you meant to me, you wouldn't have believed it. I'd given you no foundation on which to ever believe."

"I bet that revelation petrified you," she said, realizing she understood this man better than he even understood himself. She waited for the rest, relieved that he wasn't leaving and that this was probably the moment she'd been waiting for ever since meeting him.

"Terribly." Jeff reached for her, but Tori remained firm. "You want the whole shebang and you shouldn't settle for me if I'm not that. I love you enough to realize that if I've lost you, I should let you go."

His words made her insides quiver. "I do want love,

Jeff. Loving someone means that sometimes you get hurt. But it also means that you can get through anything because the end result is worth it. I love you, Jeff. All of you. Your quirks. Your job. But I need to know you love me, too."

"I've been in love with you the entire time," Jeff said. "Ever since your pregnancy it's as if someone's been hitting me on the head trying to knock sense into me. I love you, Tori, and I'm prepared to fight for you as long as I have to."

"And if I hadn't loved you back?"

"Then I would have been lonely," Jeff said, "because I would've lost the most important thing in the world to me. You."

At that moment she wanted nothing more than to throw herself in his arms, but she waited, sensing he wasn't through.

"I'm going to spend the rest of my life making you believe I love you," Jeff said. Once he finally got the box open, he knew he wouldn't be able to tuck anything back in. She placed her hand on his arm.

He shook his head and took a deep breath. "I've never said those words to anyone else," he said.

"I kind of figured that," Tori said, her heart beginning to overflow with joy. "You can say them to me every day from here forward if you'd like."

"I love you, Tori Adams. More than you'll ever know."

"I love you, Jeff Wright." Happiness consumed her. She reached for him and drew his hands into hers. "Our hearts have always been in the right place. And tonight was about blasting down those walls."

He brought his lips down to hers.

She leaned into him, her mouth joining his. She

didn't just lose herself in this kiss—this time she found herself as well. She'd changed. Jeff had changed. They loved each other. Their future was limitless.

"I love you," he said again. "If I told you that I still intend to marry you and make this love of ours official, would that be okay?"

"You'll have to ask me," Tori said.

Jeff smiled. "I will," he said, "when the moment's right. That is something I want to be perfect."

THAT MOMENT already had been perfect, but Tori had to admit that being asked on Christmas morning, with Jeff down on bended knee in front of his entire family, was more perfect.

She no longer doubted that he loved her.

"Congratulations," Lauren said, moving to stop Hailey from dropping a strand of beads around Brendan's neck. Brendan was in his bouncy seat, secure on the kitchen counter, and Hailey had used a chair to get a good look at her cousin.

"Thanks," Tori said. "I guess we both got the Wright men."

Lauren laughed as she glanced over to where Justin was talking with his brother in the great room. "You know, I think we did." She scooped up Hailey and took her to her father.

Jeff appeared then. "Having fun?"

"Yeah," Tori said. "I'm very happy."

"I'm glad," Jeff said. He leaned down to kiss her long and hard. "I'm planning on making you happy for the rest of your days."

"I like the sound of that," she said.

"Just tell me when," he said.

"How about we get married in February?"

"I'd say that's not soon enough," Jeff said, giving her a long kiss before his mother came in, beaming.

Tori laughed as Jeff went to attend to his family. As she grabbed the chips to refill the bowl, her phone rang. She picked it up.

"Merry Christmas," three voices shouted.

"We're all on conference call," Lisa said.

"We've all been so busy that we haven't been able to catch up," Cecile confirmed.

"We couldn't wait any longer to hear your news. So what's going on? Do tell," Lisa yelled.

Jeff came back and planted a kiss on Tori's neck. She handed him the bag of chips. "Shoo," she told him.

"Is he right there?" Lisa asked.

"Yes," Tori said.

"Are things better? You didn't call us," Cecile said. "We've been dying here."

"I planned on calling. It's only been two weeks."

"So spill," Joann said.

Jeff had put the chips down and came and wrapped his arms around Tori. In his bouncy seat, Brendan was waving his fist in front of his face.

Tori glanced at Jeff. His emotions were written all over his face for everyone to see; Tori had no difficulty observing the love he felt for her. "Lisa, Joann and Cecile," Tori said, humor and seriousness lacing her voice, "what are you all doing in February? And, Joann, I don't care how big you're getting because I'm not waiting any longer. You see, the order's changed again. Sorry girls, but, Cecile, I'm next."

And as Jeff kissed her earlobe and the girls shrieked their congratulations through the phone, Tori decided that life was finally exactly the way it should be.

* * * * *

Set in darkness beyond the ordinary world.
Passionate tales of life and death.
With characters' lives ruled by laws the
everyday world can't begin to imagine.

n●cturne

It's time to discover the Raintree trilogy...

New York Times bestselling author
LINDA HOWARD
brings you the dramatic first book
RAINTREE: INFERNO

The Ansara Wizards are rising and the Raintree clan
must rejoin the battle against their foes, testing their
powers, relationships and forcing upon them lives
they never could have imagined before...

Turn the page for a sneak preview
of the captivating first book
in the Raintree trilogy,
RAINTREE: INFERNO
by LINDA HOWARD
On sale April 2

$\mathbf{D}$ante Raintree stood with his arms crossed as he watched the woman on the monitor. The image was in black and white to better show details; color distracted the brain. He focused on her hands, watching every move she made, but what struck him most was how uncommonly *still* she was. She didn't fidget or play with her chips, or look around at the other players. She peeked once at her down card, then didn't touch it again, signaling for another hit by tapping a fingernail on the table. Just because she didn't seem to be paying attention to the other players, though, didn't mean she was as unaware as she seemed.

"What's her name?" Dante asked.

"Lorna Clay," replied his chief of security, Al Rayburn.

"At first I thought she was counting, but she doesn't pay enough attention."

"She's paying attention, all right," Dante murmured. "You just don't see her doing it." A card counter had to remember every card played. Supposedly counting cards was impossible with the number of decks used by the casinos, but there were those rare individuals who could calculate the odds even with multiple decks.

"I thought that, too," said Al. "But look at this piece of tape coming up. Someone she knows comes up to her and speaks, she looks around and starts chatting, completely misses the play of the people to her left—and doesn't look around even when the deal comes back to her, just taps that finger. And damn if she didn't win. Again."

Dante watched the tape, rewound it, watched it again. Then he watched it a third time. There had to be something he was missing, because he couldn't pick out a single giveaway.

"If she's cheating," Al said with something like respect, "she's the best I've ever seen."

"What does your gut say?"

Al scratched the side of his jaw, considering. Finally, he said, "If she isn't cheating, she's the luckiest person walking. She wins. Week in, week out, she wins. Never a huge amount, but I ran the numbers and she's into us for about five grand a week. Hell, boss, on her way out of the casino she'll stop by a slot machine, feed a dollar in and walk away with at least fifty. It's never the same machine, either. I've had her watched, I've had her followed, I've even looked for the same faces in the casino every time she's in here, and I can't find a common denominator."

"Is she here now?"

"She came in about half an hour ago. She's playing blackjack, as usual."

"Bring her to my office," Dante said, making a swift decision. "Don't make a scene."

"Got it," said Al, turning on his heel and leaving the security center.

Dante left, too, going up to his office. His face was

calm. Normally he would leave it to Al to deal with a cheater, but he was curious. How was she doing it? There were a lot of bad cheaters, a few good ones, and every so often one would come along who was the stuff of which legends were made: the cheater who didn't get caught, even when people were alert and the camera was on him—or, in this case, her.

It was possible to simply be lucky, as most people understood luck. Chance could turn a habitual loser into a big-time winner. Casinos, in fact, thrived on that hope. But luck itself wasn't habitual, and he knew that what passed for luck was often something else: cheating. And there was the other kind of luck, the kind he himself possessed, but it depended not on chance but on who and what he was. He knew it was an innate power and not Dame Fortune's erratic smile. Since power like his was rare, the odds made it likely the woman he'd been watching was merely a very clever cheat.

Her skill could provide her with a very good living, he thought, doing some swift calculations in his head. Five grand a week equaled $260,000 a year, and that was just from his casino. She probably hit them all, careful to keep the numbers relatively low so she stayed under the radar.

He wondered how long she'd been taking him, how long she'd been winning a little here, a little there, before Al noticed.

The curtains were open on the wall-to-wall window in his office, giving the impression, when one first opened the door, of stepping out onto a covered balcony. The glazed window faced west, so he could catch the sunsets. The sun was low now, the sky painted in purple and gold. At his home in the mountains, most of the windows faced east, affording him views of the sunrise. Something in him needed both the greeting and the goodbye of the sun. He'd always been drawn to sunlight, maybe because fire was his element to call, to control.

He checked his internal time: four minutes until sundown. Without checking the sunrise tables every day, he knew exactly when the sun would slide behind the mountains. He didn't own an alarm clock. He didn't need one. He was so acutely attuned to the sun's position that he had only to check within himself to know the time. As for waking at a particular time, he was one of those people who could tell himself to wake at a certain time, and he did. That talent had nothing to do with being Raintree, so he didn't have to hide it; a lot of perfectly ordinary people had the same ability.

He had other talents and abilities, however, that did require careful shielding. The long days of summer instilled in him an almost sexual high, when he could feel contained power buzzing just beneath his skin. He had to be doubly careful not to cause candles to leap into flame just by his presence, or to start wildfires with a glance in the dry-as-tinder brush. He loved Reno; he didn't want to burn it down. He just felt so damn *alive* with all the sunshine pouring down that he wanted to let the energy pour through him instead of holding it inside.

This must be how his brother Gideon felt while pulling lightning, all that hot power searing through his muscles, his veins. They had this in common, the connection with raw power. All the members of the far-flung Raintree clan had some power, some heightened ability, but only members of the royal family could channel and control the earth's natural energies.

Dante wasn't just of the royal family, he was the Dranir, the leader of the entire clan. "Dranir" was synonymous with king, but the position he held wasn't ceremonial, it was one of sheer power. He was the oldest son of the previous Dranir, but he would have been passed over for the position if he hadn't also inherited the power to hold it.

Behind him came Al's distinctive knock on the door. The outer office was empty, Dante's secretary having gone home hours before. "Come in," he called, not turning from his view of the sunset.

The door opened, and Al said, "Mr. Raintree, this is Lorna Clay."

Dante turned and looked at the woman, all his senses on alert. The first thing he noticed was the vibrant color of her hair, a rich, dark red that encompassed a multitude of shades from copper to burgundy. The warm amber light danced along the iridescent strands, and he felt a hard tug of sheer lust in his gut. Looking at her hair was almost like looking at fire, and he had the same reaction.

The second thing he noticed was that she was spitting mad.

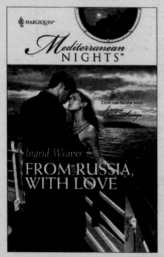

Silhouette®

ROMANTIC SUSPENSE

**Sparked by Danger,
Fueled by Passion.**

*This month and every month look for
four new heart-racing romances
set against a backdrop of suspense!*

Available in May 2007

Safety in Numbers
(*Wild West Bodyguards miniseries*)
by Carla Cassidy

Jackson's Woman
by Maggie Price

Shadow Warrior
(*Night Guardians miniseries*)
by Linda Conrad

One Cool Lawman
by Diane Pershing

Available wherever you buy books!

Visit Silhouette Books at www.eHarlequin.com   SRS0407

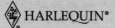
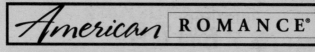

REQUEST YOUR FREE BOOKS!
2 FREE NOVELS PLUS 2
FREE GIFTS!

American **R O M A N C E**®

Heart, Home & Happiness!

YES! Please send me 2 FREE Harlequin American Romance® novels and my 2 FREE gifts. After receiving them, if I don't wish to receive any more books, I can return the shipping statement marked "cancel." If I don't cancel, I will receive 4 brand-new novels every month and be billed just $4.24 per book in the U.S., or $4.99 per book in Canada, plus 25¢ shipping and handling per book and applicable taxes, if any*. That's a savings of close to 15% off the cover price! I understand that accepting the 2 free books and gifts places me under no obligation to buy anything. I can always return a shipment and cancel at any time. Even if I never buy another book from Harlequin, the two free books and gifts are mine to keep forever.

154 HDN EEZK   354 HDN EEZV

Name	(PLEASE PRINT)
Address	Apt. #
City	State/Prov.	Zip/Postal Code

Signature (if under 18, a parent or guardian must sign)

Mail to the **Harlequin Reader Service®:**
IN U.S.A.: P.O. Box 1867, Buffalo, NY 14240-1867
IN CANADA: P.O. Box 609, Fort Erie, Ontario L2A 5X3

Not valid to current Harlequin American Romance subscribers.

Want to try two free books from another line?
Call 1-800-873-8635 or visit www.morefreebooks.com.

* Terms and prices subject to change without notice. NY residents add applicable sales tax. Canadian residents will be charged applicable provincial taxes and GST. This offer is limited to one order per household. All orders subject to approval. Credit or debit balances in a customer's account(s) may be offset by any other outstanding balance owed by or to the customer. Please allow 4 to 6 weeks for delivery.

Your Privacy: Harlequin is committed to protecting your privacy. Our Privacy Policy is available online at www.eHarlequin.com or upon request from the Reader Service. From time to time we make our lists of customers available to reputable firms who may have a product or service of interest to you. If you would prefer we not share your name and address, please check here. ☐

HAR07

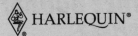

HARLEQUIN®

American ROMANCE®

COMING NEXT MONTH

www.eHarlequin.com

HARCNM0407